# Buried Echoes

Liam Bevan

# Contents

# Prologue

The hot sun blazes down on the small island of San Mahina, the only relief from the sweltering heat being the ocean breeze blowing in from the Atlantic and the small amount of shade offered by the numerous palm trees.

White, sandy beaches wrap around the small island with the occasional rocks and boulders splattered across the shore line. San Mahina is lunar shaped, with the north side of the island facing the vast Atlantic Ocean, large waves crashing against the shore. The south side of the island is more lagoon-like with deep, blue waters often patrolled by fishermen and divers.

Not far from the British Virgin Islands, San Mahina's climate is very tropical. Various warm weather fruits are harvested from the island's many acres of farm land, sustaining the island's economy.

In the beginning, in the early twentieth century, the island boomed with tourists. People would come from all over to see San Mahina's cristal blue waters and white sands, but its cerulean depths that seemed so beautiful and mesmerizing, could be quite deceiving.

In 1927, a sixty-four year old man went fishing on the south side of the island. The man was missing for two days before he washed ashore, but a victim of drowning, he was not. Portions of his skin had been mercilessly torn from his body, not from the teeth of a shark, but skillfully done by the hand of a monster.

Later, in 1936, two young men went swimming on the west corner of the island. One of the men watched as his companion was dragged into the water by his ankles, never to be seen again. The witness could only describe the monster as being just a shadow in the waves.

In 1942, a woman drowned in front of her newly wedded husband. In 1954, a local man was pulled out of his boat only to wash up on shore without any arms. 1963 had two swimmers dead within six months. The number of attacks kept rising, and the island's inhabitants began to decline.

By the 1990s, San Mahina was nearly abandoned, the only residents being the locals and the occasional renter. No longer were the days of happy vacations and sunny retreats. The once crystalline blue water would forever be red in the haunted minds of those who witnessed the island's horrors.

And so the palm trees continued to sway in false security, the island forever haunted by its cerulean depths. There were never any survivors of the attacks, but there were witnesses.

And they all described the monster as the same.

A shadow in the sea.

# Chapter 1

- - - - - - - - - - - - - - - - - - - - - - - - - - - - - - - - - - - - - - - - - -

On one of San Mahina's many avenues, in front of a small booth, under the awning away from the sun, stands a young woman. She is clad in ripped shorts and a thin tank top over a maroon swimsuit. Her thick, blonde hair is pulled back into a loose pony tail, a few strands sticking to her sweaty forehead.

She meanders through the stand's products, her gaze falling on a basket of mangos. Her long fingers graze over the fruits, swatting the occasional bug. Her grey eyes glance up, signaling with her hand for the seller.

The short man shuffles over, his deeply tanned skin proving he is a local. He smiles at the young woman, wrinkles forming around his eyes.

"Would you like to check out, miss?" He asks, an accent audible in his words.

"Yes, sir," the young woman replies politely, a small smile gracing her thin lips. "These two mangos," she says, handing the man the fruits.

She follows the man as he leads her to a table with a cash register. The man scrutinizes her curiously, his eyebrows furrowing. "You are not from here, are you?" He asks, no doubt noticing her pale skin and blonde hair from a climate much cooler than the island.

"No, sir. I'm on vacation with my family," she replies, handing him the appropriate cash.

The man frowns. "We don't get many tourists here anymore."

"It is a shame, isn't it? This place is beautiful," the girl replies airily, smiling at the sight of a small bird flying past.

"You mean to say you do not know?" He asks.

"I don't follow, sir."

The older fellow lowers his voice, gesturing her to incline her ear. The girl obliges, though not without much wary hesitance. "There are legends, miss--stories."

"What kind of stories?" She questions.

"Drownings! Unexplainable disappearances," he murmurs. "You ask why no one comes here. Aye, for good reason they don't! No one goes in those waters and comes back alive."

"Sir, I'm sorry but--"

The man shakes his head frantically. "No, no, miss. Don't go in the water, miss. Dangerous things swim those waters."

"Don't listen to him. He's a crazy old man," a woman at a neighboring stand says, scrutinizing the man with her nose upturned.

Disregarding the woman's cruel remark, and feeling a need to spare the man's feelings, she asks: "What dangerous things?"

The man looks both ways, shooting the other woman a dark look, before returning his gaze to the girl.

"There are many tales and legends of what could be in those waters, no one knows for sure, but I can tell you what I believe," the man whispers, his eyes grazing the people passing by.

The girl feels like she is in some clandestine meeting by his secretive tone. She waits impatiently for him to continue.

"I did not believe the tales either, at first. Some drownings date back as far as the 1600s, after all, but then I saw it first-hand."

The woman's eyes widen in shock. Saw it with his own eyes?

"My brother. He was... taken," he says solemnly.

"I'm so sorry, sir," she says, sympathy evident in her tone.

He waves a hand dismissively. "Not to worry, it was long ago. Now, as I was saying: we had gone for a swim on the southern side of the island. It was sunny and the water was extremely clear, which was how I was able to see what took him."

The young woman kneads her hands in anticipation as he continues. "He was just a few paces in front of me, standing on the outer edge of the sandbar. Normally, it was safe on the sandbar, but not this time.

"I saw a red tail nearly six feet long, and before I had a chance to warn him, my brother was already screaming. 'Something has my leg!' He had said. I ran for him but his fingers slip through my grasp!" The man throws his arms high in the air in a gesture, making the girl jump. "He was gone the next moment," the man struggles to finish his sentence. "There was only a bit of blood left in the water where he had just been standing."

A shuddering breath escapes the woman's parted lips. She wasn't expecting such a gruesome story. Her head snaps back in the man's direction as he continues his story.

"Just before he went out of sight, I caught a glimpse of thing that took him. The red tail was there, yes," A crazed look takes over the man's features. "But a human body was at the other end. He was man and fish."

The other woman's warning from earlier pops back into her mind, her face taking on a skeptical look.

"Sir, I'm sure what you saw could not have be--"

"I do not lie, miss," he says, his voice rising. "I know what I saw!"

"I-I should get going, sir. Thanks for telling me," she says shakily, grabbing the bag of mangos from him, starting to fear his sudden outburst.

"No, please listen. I'm not crazy. I know what I saw!" The man yells as she hastily scurries away down the street.

What was she thinking? What did she expect? A large fish or a shark infestation maybe, but not this!

The young woman continues her fast pace down the street, unsure if she is running from the crazed man, or the story he told her.

Finally out of the village, the woman slows her pace to a leisurely walk. Her feet are aching from the many miles of gravelly streets covered just in a pair of sandals. She rounds the bend in the road, the bungalow her family is renting coming into view.

It is rather beachy looking with its vertical wooden siding and faux thatched roof. A small porch wraps around the exterior with steps leading to the main door and the private boardwalk.

Thoughts of her conversation with the village man cloud the young woman's mind. What did he really see? He was drowned, albeit not by a mermaid, but by something, that's for sure. Just what exactly was it? Either way, the water is probably dangerous.

"We were almost worried about you, Cally. You have been gone for hours," the girl's mother says to her as she steps into the bungalow.

"Sorry, I lost track of time," she replies, setting the bag of mangos on the kitchen counter. "I got some mangos."

"Ooh, mangos? Yum!" Cally's eight year old brother, Ethan, says, running into the kitchen.

"I also met a village man. He told me an interesting story," Cally says.

"What kind of story?" Her father asks from the sitting room where he is perched on the couch next to her mother.

"Well...it was about a drowning, actually," Cally says hesitantly. She isn't quite sure how they will react to hearing this strange tale.

"Really? Well, let's hear it, then. Probably bogus anyways," her dad says offhandedly.

Cally relays the information to her eager family, leaving out the part about it possibly being a mermaid.

"And then a giant fish just pulled him into the water," she finishes.

"Maybe there is something out there..." her mother ponders.

"Nah, even if there is--which I highly doubt--there are a lot of people on this island. The chances of it attacking one of us is slim," Cally's father says.

"I suppose you are right," her mom replies.

"Are you sure?" Ethan asks a scared look marring his boyish features.

"Yes, sweety, there is nothing to worry about," her mom assures him with a smile. Maybe there isn't anything to worry about. I can trust my parents' judgement, right? Cally asks herself.

"Hey, I'm going to go down to the beach really quick. I will be back in a minute," Cally says before heading to the door.

"Alright, but be back in time for dinner!" She hears her mom say before the door closes. Cally sighs, trotting down the steps. This probably wasn't the best vacation spot. Mysterious drownings? A monster in the sea?

The bugs chirp endlessly as Cally makes her way down the board-walk. Once she reaches the sand though, the sound of the loud bugs are replaced by the soothing crashing of the waves.

The sun has set on the horizon, but the sky is still painted a pinkish orange along the western corner of the island. The cold sand under her feet mixed with the gentle breeze cause goosebumps to appear on her pale skin.

Today was a good first day of vacation, she decides. She is still afraid of the water, that's for sure. This doesn't stop her from walking close enough for the waves to crash against her shins, though.

Cally wraps her arms around herself as she watches the sky get darker and darker, the waves only just visible. Out of the corner of her eye, she sees a large splash in the water. Her eyes widen as a long, black tail rises up out of the murky depths, it's dark scales glistening in the moonlight.

Just as soon as it appears, it is gone, splashing back into the sea. Cally shivers at what it could have been. She has never seen such a tail before. With a sigh, she turns around and trudges back through the sand towards the bungalow.

She was never aware of the pair of obsidian eyes watching her from the dark waters.

# Chapter 2

Cally stirs in her sleep as a gentle breeze caresses her exposed skin from the open window. A sigh leaves her lips as she slowly comes to consciousness. She blearily wipes her blonde hair out of her eyes and pulls herself up into a sitting position. Her gaze travels to the open window, a smile twisting up her lips at the sight before her.

Beyond the porch outside her window lay the rolling dunes. Sea oats sway as the breeze blows down the deserted beach. Crystal blue waves crash against the shore as pelicans swoop down from above, easily catching fish in their eager beaks.

She also notices that the breeze is blowing much stronger than it normally does, along with a dark strip of clouds on the horizon.

Deciding it's probably time to get up, as it's almost 8:oo, Cally stands from her reclined position, stretching her arms above her head as she does so. She pads into her en suite, humming a tune under her breath as she prepares herself a shower. She has been looking forward to this day since they first planned the trip.

Today was to be spent sailing on the south side of the island. Her parents had already rented a small sailboat for them to use on their aquatic escapade, and Cally couldn't be more excited to go out on the open ocean. Although, with the strength of the wind and the ominous clouds in the distance, perhaps they may not go.

A small voice in the back of her mind quietly whispered of the possible dangers of the water, urging her to remember the fear-stricken face of the village man. Wouldn't it be silly to push her luck? Maybe it isn't a mermaid that is stalking the island, but there is something. Cally brushes the voice aside; this was her day of fun and nothing was going to stop her from enjoying herself--not even a storm or the rumor of a flesh eating monster.

She goes about her normal morning routine, still humming the same tune. Music is a big part of Cally's life, as she spends most of her time either singing or playing her ukelele, though she never sings for others besides Ethan. Cally was far too afraid to sing to anyone else.

But yes, she has a lovely voice. She wants to write her own songs, but has never had the imagination to do so, preferring to just sing along to the artists whose songs play through the earbuds that are nearly constantly in her ears.

After her shower, she slips on a navy blue swimsuit that complements her pale complexion. It was just a simple suit with thin straps that crisscrossed over her back and attached to the strings in the back, which were tied neatly in a bow. The front was a simple, low scoop neck, something she could easily pull off with her small breasts. The bottoms weren't flashy either, just plain navy blue fabric that fit her athletic curves.

She threw a pair of ripped shorts and a loose tank top on over it and slipped sandals on her feet. With her hair still slightly damp from her shower, she leaves it down. Grabbing her water-proof camera, she leaves her room and heads to the kitchen.

The camera was a Christmas gift from her little brother. She had always liked photography, almost as much as she loved music. It didn't take the best pictures, but it was water-proof, which made it easy to take with her on her many outdoor adventures.

She enters the main living area to see Ethan already up and ready to go, no doubt just as excited for today as Cally is. He wears sunglasses perched low on his little nose and a floppy hat adorns his head. He hasn't noticed her yet, as he is busy checking out his arms as he flexes them.

"Whatcha doing, bud?" Cally questions with an amused smile on her lips.

"Oh, hi, Cally. Look at this shirt!" He says, gesturing to his muscle shirt with a Minion on it. "It has no sleeves, so you can see my muscles!" At that, he flexes his little noodle arms, clearly seeing more muscle than what is actually there.

"Uh huh," she mumbles at his silly antics as she heads to the cabinet to fetch some cereal.

He is a rather rambunctious little boy, and would sometimes get on her nerves when he disrupted her quiet, but she probably loved him more than both of her parents combined.

It's not that she didn't love her parents, but she never quite clicked with them. They just didn't understand her quirky, introverted nature. Ethan, on the other hand, was amazed by anything she did. He would listen to her play music and demand she perform mini concerts for him, and in turn, she would always cheer for him at his little league baseball games.

"Have you eaten yet, little bud?" She asked. She never called him by his first name, unless she was mad at him, that is.

He shrugs. "I forgot."

She chuckles a bit, grabbing two bowls from the cabinet and setting them on the bar and pulling out a stool. "Here, you might want to eat before the trip. Don't want you to get hungry half way through and have your stomach ruin your day."

A flash of horror crosses his face. "No, that won't happen. I'll eat."

She chuckles again as he greedily snatches the Lucky Charms from her and pours himself a heaping serving. The two chat animatedly back and forth, smiles on their faces as they eat their Lucky Charms.

If only she knew it would be the last meal they had together for a very, very long time.

The walk to the marina isn't a long one, only about a mile. Cally spent the entire time staring up at the sky, almost willing the dark clouds to go away. Maybe it was childish to act as she was, but she ignored the thought.

By the time they reach the marina, the sun is almost at its peak. According to Cally's watch, its 11:43 a.m. The family ventures down the dock to their destination: a small dock with rows and rows of rentable sailboats.

They enter a small shop, a bell ringing at their entry. The atmosphere was clearly geared towards fisherman with all of the fishing equipment and bait. Cally scrunches her nose at the unfamiliar stench of raw fish.

She vaguely hears her father talking to the man behind the desk as she meanders through the shop, her fingers occasionally brushing some of the merchandise.

"Alright! Y'all ready to go?" Cally's father says excitedly, raising a small pair of keys in his hand, jingling them.

"Are you sure? The storm looks a little rough..." her mother says, squinting her eyes at the horizon.

"Well, we can ask the locals, right? They probably deal with storms all the time," Cally suggests, nodding towards the grungy-looking man behind the counter.

"I guess so," her father says with a shrug of his thin shoulders.

He approaches the counter, looking entirely out of place with his khakis and over the top Hawaiian T-shirt. The man never looked up from his magazine.

"We were just wondering if, as a local, you thought the storm was too rough to go sailing in? We were looking and weren't su--"

"You'll be fine," the man says, cutting him off.

"Oh! Uh, alright then. Have a great day, sir!"

The man grunts in response, flipping the page of his magazine. Cally's father turns around, shrugging his shoulders.

"Guess we are alright, then."

The small family makes their way out to the dock, looking for a boat with the number 29 on its side.

"Is that one it?" Ethan asks, jogging over to a small, white sailboat with 29 stamped on its side in red.

"Probably," Cally says.

The boat really is small, only about sixteen feet in length. As her father busies with the sails and trolling motor, Cally watches the ocean before her, unable to shake the feeling that something very, very bad would happen.

# Chapter 3

The boat rocks unsteadily in the waves, its top heavy mast pivoting back and forth in the wind. Cally's mother sits next to Ethan while Cally and her father reel in the sail. After about an hour on the water, there was a unanimous vote to stow the sail and use the small motor to drive back to shore. The wind had picked up exponentially, what was once a steady breeze had become a harsh wind. With the winds, the waves had also increased.

"That should do it," her father says as he ties the final strap over the mast, its once billowing sail now tied securely to the frame.

"This was a terrible idea," Cally mutters dejectedly.

"At least it won't take us too long to get back, right? That's the shore, isn't it? Only about three miles out?" Her mother says, almost worriedly.

"Don't worry, I got this. We will be back in no time," her father says cheerfully, but Cally can hear the slight tremble to his words.

He starts the motor with ease, the small boat slicing through the waves as it starts its journey back to the dock. The motor isn't a large one, they probably aren't going much faster than about ten miles per hour, but it's better than nothing.

Cally shuffles closer to her brother and wraps a towel around the two of them. The sky has darkened considerably and, combined with the wind, has dropped the temperature quite a few degrees. She tries to ignore the worried look on her father's face as the storm continues to come towards them at a faster pace than the boat, the dark line of clouds only a couple of miles out.

"We probably shouldn't have come out this far," Cally says, voicing her concerns. Her mother pins her father with an accusing stare.

"Well, I wasn't really expecting the storm..." he says, avoiding eye contact.

Cally sighs; she supposes he is right. The man from the marina did say they would be fine. Then again, Cally has had a feeling this day wouldn't go well, no matter how hard she tried to ignore it.

Ever since she heard what the village man had to say, something has been nagging at the back of her mind, begging--pleading--to be heard. Quiet whispers in the back of her mind urging her to stay away from the water.

As the waves start to crash over the front of the bow, Cally realizes she should have listened to the voices--should have listened to their pleads to stay away--to run. Fear spreads through Cally's system as her instincts tell her this is wrong. This won't end well.

A loud clap of thunder sounds, frightening the small family. A small cry escapes Ethan's lips as more thunder rumbles, the occasional bolt visible among the clouds. Cally pulls her brother closer to her side.

"The owner did say life jackets were in the bench, right?" Cally hears her father asks.

"Yes, why?" She replies, eager to have the safety of a life jacket around her.

"Because there is only one in here."

Cally whips her head around to face him. "What do you mean?"

"I mean, there is only one jacket, that's it."

"There has to be others somewhere," her mom says, quickly standing to search through every nook and cranny of the small boat. Cally begins to fear the storm more and more as no others are found.

"Here, you take it," her mother says, handing the life jacket to Ethan. He hesitantly puts it on, the adult large easily swallowing his tiny frame.

The boat continues rock unsteadily on the waves as the surf gets higher and higher. The strong gale whips around the little boat, Cally's hair blowing into her face.

Her eyes scan the horizon as the storm looms closer, the haze of rain now visible. She can hear it before it hits, the pattering of rain on the ocean's surface filling her ears as the rain drops begin to soak through her clothes. Goosebumps travel up her arms as the cool precipitation settles on her skin.

Thunder erupts once more through the sky as the rain continues to come down harder and harder. The rolling swells are now at least 6 feet high, the boat bouncing around on the water like a spinning top, the motor doing it's best to keep them going in a straight line.

"Are we even getting closer?" Cally shouts over the sound of the heavy rain.

"I-I… no, we aren't," her father stammers, a fearful look on his face.

"What do you mean we aren't getting closer?!" Her mom nearly shouts.

"The current is pushing us out just as fast as we are driving in!"

Ethan starts to cry as the boat crashes over another wave, water spraying over the bow and soaking Cally to her bones.

"Do something, Jared!" Cally's mother shouts at her father.

"Do what? Paddle?" He snaps back as he struggles to aim the nose of the boat into the waves.

Cally grips the side of the boat with one hand and holds her brother tightly to her side with the other. Fear creeps up her spine as the boat rises and falls with the growing swells. Her muscles tense as she struggles to remain calm under the circumstances.

As the little boat rises up on another wave, Cally's gaze is drawn to splash in the water a few meters away. A black tail rises up out of the water before splashing back down into the raging sea.

She recognizes that tail.

It was the same tail she saw while standing on the beach that night. An extreme sense of foreboding and fear settles in her bones, her breaths becoming shallow pants as she eyes the spot where the creature once was.

"Dad?" She mumbles shakily. "Dad we need to get back, now," she says, this time more audible. She isn't sure where her fear is coming from, but she knew it was about time she started trusting her instincts.

"I'm trying, sweety!" He yells over the storm.

"Dad please!" She nearly screams as the boat turns sideways.

The village man's words echo in her head like an endless chant. Over and over again the same words repeat themselves in her brain.

"I saw a tail nearly six feet long..."

"Nothing left but a pool of blood..."

This time she sees the tail, it is closer. Its black scales glint in the light of a lightning strike like shining armour. Her heart thunders in her chest as the black fins sink back into the water where it hides, taunting her with its mystery.

"Did you guys see that?" She says.

None of them seem to hear her.

More water crashes down on them both from the rain and the raging sea. The boat is nearly flooded from the many waves that have crashed over its sides. By now both her mother and Ethan are crying, their pale faces reflecting the fear on Cally's own face.

"The steering's not working!" Jared shouts as he struggles to turn the boat to its rightful position.

Despite his efforts, the boat turns sideways, its flat sides facing the onslaught of crashing waves. One of the largest swells she has seen so far comes towards them, its peak at least twelve feet tall. With the bow not heading straight into the wave, the small boat will easily flip.

Cally jumps into the fray, helping her father to steer the boat back into the correct position. Their efforts prove to be futile as the boat only stays in the same position, almost as if something were holding it in place...

Cally faintly hears her mother scream as the wave climbs higher and higher, closer and closer. Cally latches onto her brother, her nails practically digging into his skin as she desperately holds onto him.

The boat is pulled towards it as the swell sucks in the surrounding water. A white cap forms on the crest. The wave arches down...

The wave's peak crashes straight into the middle of the boat, a wall of white slamming into the boat's occupants. The water first slams Cally into the bottom of the boat befor it flips entirely, Cally being tossed around with it, her hold on Ethan long gone.

Different things crash into her at all angles. Wood. Fiberglass. Skin. Metal. Water invades her senses, her nose, eyes and throat burning as liquid forces itself into her body. She screams into the water as she is compressed, tossed, flipped through the raging sea, no longer knowing which way is up.

Cally forces herself to kick her legs, urging body to fight back against the treacherous ocean. She kicks, claws for the surface, her body aching but her mind ignoring it, the adrenaline in her system pushing the pain aside.

Finally, her hand breaches the surface of the water, her head and shoulders quickly following. Her eyes sting as she opens them, her lungs barely catching a breath before she is crushed by another wave.

Kicking back to the surface, she sputters and coughs between eager inhales. She whips her head back and forth, searching for any of her family. She spots the boat in the distance and she desperately swims to its upturned form. Its tiny motor and rutter stick in the air like a flag.

Through the relentless crashes of waves and crackles of lightning, she reaches the sailboat. She claws desperately for anything to grab onto on its smooth surface. She latches onto the rutter, refusing to let go as another wave washes over her.

"C-Cally?" A voice says. Her head whips around to find her parents pulling themselves onto the boat on the other side.

"Mom!" She practically sobs, her tears mixing with the rain and ocean around her.

"Where's Ethan?" Cally mumbles. "Mom, where is Ethan?" She says louder this time.

"I-I don't know!"

"Ethan!" Cally screams into the torrents of wind and rain. "Ethan!"

"Cally!" She hears behind her. She looks back to see her little brother barely keeping his head above water as the life vest has floated up over his shoulders.

Without thinking, Cally releases her hold on the boat and swims out to her brother. A giant wave crashes over her and she flips under the water. Kicking back to the surface, she scans the water for her brother. The boat is still behind her, though much farther away now.

Before she can spin back around, a little hand is latching onto her shoulder.

"Cally," Ethan sobs as he practically crawls onto her shoulders.

"Ethan you have to let go I can't swim with you on my back," she instructs. Kicking her legs in an effort to keep them above the crashing waves.

"Just put your hand on my shoulder." Ethan does as he is told, his little body shaking with fear and exhaustion.

The brother and sister swim their way back to the boat, their limbs aching and their lungs burning. The waves and rain are a continuous onslaught as they pull themselves onto the boat's upturned hull.

"Are you two alright?" Jared asks them. Cally only manages a nod as another wave splashes over them.

Cally's face pales, her heart thudding in her chest, her fingers tightening around the rutter. There, just behind her parents was another splash--the tail again. It was hardly ten feet from them. It almost seems as if the creature is haunting her.

"What was that, Cally?" Ethan asks shakily.

"Its going to be okay," she says, avoiding his question.

Her mother's shrill scream startles Cally and she whips her head to the side. Her mother raises a shaking finger and points behind Cally.

"Mom, what is it?" She shouts just before another wave crashes, rocking the upturned boat.

"I don't know. It was--it was--" she sobs, latching onto her husband.

"Everyone get on the boat. Whatever it is, we don't want it to attack us!" Her father shouts over the wind and rain, his curly hair plastered to his forehead.

As Cally's parents struggle to climb the rocking, upturned sailboat on the other side, Cally helps her brother on their side. Water rains down on them like pellets of ice, nearly stinging her skin with the force. Her body ignores the harsh stabs of pain in her abdomen as she shoves her brother onto the ship's hull.

After he has safely climbed on top, albeit sliding around as if he were on ice, Cally climbs up behind him, taking her father's outstretched hand. Just as her body is completely out of the water, a harsh grip latches onto her ankle, tugging her back into the sea.

Cally screams as she nearly loses her father's grip. She kicks her legs as hard as she can, her heel catching tender flesh before the grip on her ankle loosens. She frantically scrambles back onto the hull, her body refusing to acknowledge the pain.

She whips around to see the head and shoulders of a man sinking back into the water, black hair disappearing under the waves.

"Was that--"

"A man?" Her father finishes.

"H-how?" Her mother cries. "That's not possible!"

Cally's shoulders shake as barely repressed sobs rack her body. Her bleeding fingernails grip the small ridges of the boat's underbelly, her bleeding body barely holding on.

A loud, unnatural hiss has her rolling over, her legs pushing her up higher on the hull. There, grasping the edge of the boat with long, black claws, is a man. But he can't be a man--no.

Sharp claws lead to long, webbed fingers. Her gaze travels up pale, muscled arms to a neck with strange slits on the side, all the way up to the horrifying gaze of an inhuman creature. Obsidian eyes stare back at her before his lips peel back to reveal razor sharp teeth. Lightning flashes behind them, its light reflecting off the creature's wet skin.

She faintly hears the screams and cries of her family as she remains frozen in her spot. The creature uses its claws to drag itself further up the hull, closer and closer. The thing that horrifies Cally the most is the long, black fish's tail that is attached to the thing's body.

He has no legs--no. Only an obsidian black tail that spreads gracefully behind him. She knows that tail. The man's lips pull back in a hiss, revealing the two rows of sharp teeth the flicker violently in the flashes of lightning. His eyes shine with unrestrained malice before his eyes lock on Cally's. An emotion crosses the creature's face but it is quickly erased before Cally can identify it.

As the creature gets within three feet of her, Cally finds herself unfrozen. She scrambles backwards, her bare feet slipping on the slick surface. Her very bones shake with terror as the creature gets closer and closer, the rain and crashing waves creating an image she will never forget.

She chokes on unintelligible pleas as the monster looms closer still. Her father's hands grasp her shoulders, holding her from falling back down.

The village man wasn't wrong. He wasn't crazy. He was telling the truth. There are monsters in the sea. Horrid, vicious monsters with sharp teeth and claws. Cally kicks her feet at the creature.

It let's out a hiss as her heel catches its jaw, its face jerking to the side harshly. The creature slides back into the water and disappears. Cally sighs in relief, but too soon.

Cally cries out as the monster's clawed hand latches onto her ankle, having launched itself out of the water with its powerful tail. He pulls himself up higher, grasping onto the knee of her other leg.

Cally kicks and screams, her body thrashing in the monster's grip. As another wave crashes over them, her father's hands slip, letting her fall into the monster's embrace. Cally and the monster slide down the boat, the screams of her family loud in her ears before she is submerged under the waves.

Water instantly invades her senses. Her eyes sting, her lungs and nose burning. She thrashes, kicks, claws--anything to get away. Her efforts go to waste as her body slowly starts to shut down, the air in her lungs quickly being replaced by sea water.

Cally is vaguely aware of arms wrapping around her waist and behind her head before she loses consciousness, submerged in darkness.

And so she is taken.

Another victim of the mysterious sea.

# Chapter 4

P ain.

Cold.

Wet.

Those were the only things Cally's half concious mind were able to register. Panic settles in her like a spirit possessing her body, its ice cold fingers wrapping around her spine. Cally forces her eyelids open, her eyes widening. Multiple stalactites stare back at her like spears ready to pierce her soft flesh.

Harsh coughs suddenly rattle her weak frame. She doubles over, sea water dribbling down her chin as it forces it's way out of her lungs. Her ribs feel like knives are being stabbed into them with each shuddering cough. She bites her tongue to keep from crying out.

As the coughs finally come to a stop, Cally takes in a shuddering breath. She hesitantly looks down at her abdomen to see the damage done to her during the storm.

Her tank top is ripped to shreds, blood and sand making the shirt's original color hardly identifiable. Blood. So much blood. With shaking hands, she lifts the hem of her shirt, a soft cry escaping her lips as she peels it off her skin.

The soft skin of her stomach is littered with cuts and bruises. One slash goes all the way from underneath her left breast, slowly dragging across her stomach in a jagged line, all the way to the crest of her right hip. The cuts stretch and pull with every move she makes, the sand in her wounds grinding into open wounds. She is vaguely aware of a similar sting on her back.

Her gaze travels down her bare legs to see they are in similar shape, if not worse. One cut drags down the outside of her right thigh, roughly nine inches long. Other cuts litter her legs in all different directions, some deep, others shallow scrapes.

A dull ache in her hand causes her gaze to drift to her arms. Judging by the immobility of the ring and middle fingers of her left hand, Cally deduces the fingers are broken. Her arms look much like the rest of her body, her right shoulder stiff and aching, no doubt having been wrenched in an odd direction during the storm.

Too strained to remain sitting, Cally flops onto her back, her body crying out in pain as her tender spine meets hard ground. The ache in her ribs intensifies and Cally realizes she probably broke a rib or two. She is in too much pain and is too scared to feel and see if she is right.

Tears roll down her cheeks and into her hair as she stares up at the stalactites above her. She has no idea where she is. She has no idea how she got here. And above all else,

She has no idea how she is still alive.

By all accounts, she should be dead, just floating meat in an endless ocean, her body no doubt being ripped apart by sharks. Or being ripped apart by the very creature that took her. A shiver runs down her spine as she recalls the image.

Pale skin. Obsidian eyes. Long claws. Sharp teeth. A tail...

She can remember screaming. She was so afraid--so terrified. Cally wonders why--of all people--why take her? It hadn't even glanced at the rest of her family, seeming to only want her.

She is glad of that, really. She can't imagine having to see her brother be taken by the monster. She wonders how they are taking her absence. Do they think she is dead? Are they dead? Tears well in her eyes as she considers the possibility. She has survived some-how, but did they?

Cally lays on her back, softly crying as the trauma sets in. She is alive, yet alone, and with no way of knowing if the rest of her family even survived. She whimpers as she struggles to raise her hand high enough to wipe her tears, the cuts stinging and joints aching.

No. She can't just lay here like this. If her family really is dead, there is nothing she can do about it; she will assume they have safely arrived back at the island. If she is to survive, she has to do something about her current situation.

With that resolve, Cally forces herself into a sitting position. Try-ing her best to ignore the pain in her body, she casts her gaze on the cave around her. The cave is probably twelve feet high, and fifteen feet in width.

The cave's mouth opens to the sea, the entire cave submerged under the water except for the small area Cally is, at the back of the cave. The dry part where she sits is basically a half moon shape that's about ten feet from the water's edge to the back of the cave. The water rises up to her like a miniature beach.

Rocks and boulders rise from the water and litter the beach where Cally sits. Through the cave's mouth, she can see the outside, rain cascading down almost violently. It must not have been long then since she blacked out. It is getting darker though.

Eyeing the water warily, Cally decides it is the only way to cleanse her wounds. She bites her lip in trepidation. She has no idea if the creature is still there, or even if there are other creatures that could reach her if she were to get in the water. Not only that, but there is no way she could defend herself in her current state. At this rate, she won't even be able to swim out of the cave, let alone fight an underwater creature.

"I have to do it," Cally says aloud, almost as if hearing her own words will give her more courage. "Whatever it takes to survive, right?"

With that, Cally begins to drag herself into the water. She starts by swinging her legs in front of her and dipping her feet into the dark water. With the little light, she can barely see. She plants her hands by her hips and uses what little arm strength she has left to raise her pelvis off the ground and slide forwards. Scooting her feet farther out, she repeats the action, her feet now submerged up to her knees.

A soft cry sounds from her throat as she forces her body further, all the way until the water is just underneath her armpits while in the sitting position. She is too afraid to go further.

Lightheadedness causes Cally to nearly pass out, her eyelids blinking rapidly in an effort to keep herself conscious. As the dizziness passes, she sets about gently rinsing her injuries.

Tears spring into her eyes as the sand scrapes her skin as she brushes it away from her body with shaking hands. Cally carefully removes her tattered tank top and shorts, leaving her in the navy blue swimsuit. She gently squeezes the blood from the fabric before using it as a cloth to clean the rest of her body.

Once the majority of the blood and sand are gone, Cally uses the same actions as before to get back out of the water, this time in reverse. Now on dry land, she moves onto her knees.

Cally decides to create a mental checklist of her body's capabilities.

First up: standing.

She uses a nearby boulder to steady herself, the pain is so intense she nearly collapses. Cally forces herself to rise from her knees, her muscles screaming. She keeps going, knowing she will probably lose the willpower to stand if she doesn't do it now. Her legs wobble underneath her, but she succeeds in remaining standing.

Standing: Check.

Next up: Walking.

She takes in a deep breath, willing herself to not succumb to her body's pain. Mentally singing Seven Nation Army, Cally takes her first step. The bottoms of her bare feet sting as she steps on the tiny rocks that litter the ground. Her steps are wobbly and her right hip is killing her, but she is successful.

Walking: Check.

A tiny smile lifts the corners of her lips as her hands press into the cave's wall; she crossed all ten feet without falling. Not a huge feat, but to her, it's amazing. Using the wall, she lowers herself to the ground where she splays her legs out in front of her and rests her back against the hard stone.

She watches the rain outside, her eyelids slowly drooping. However she got here, she is glad its here and not out there in the rain.

With exhaustion plaguing her body, she let's her eyes shut, allowing sleep to take over.

# Chapter 5

Cally is awoken from her slumber by a low grumbling sound in her stomach. Hunger. It's quite obvious. She was probably too stunned by shock last night to take notice of the growing ache in her belly.

She leans forward, her neck and shoulders stiff from having slept leaning against the cave's wall. Her muscles ache as she forces movement in her limbs, the soreness from yesterday lingering unwelcomly. Rain no longer drizzles outside the mouth of the cave, the sun bright and shining. Its light shines on the water, reflecting off the rippling surface and onto the cave's many stalactites overhead.

Cally's attention is drawn back to food by another rumble of her stomach. Her tongue is also wanting not just for food, but also for water. Her mouth is dry and cottony from the lack of moisture, an uncomfortable feeling for sure.

Well, as neither seem to be attainable, food not being catchable in her current state of handicap and the only water available being salty, she decides on instead building a fire. Some dry warmth would be nice.

Except, there also seems to be a lack of wood as well.

No fire.

No water.

No food.

The most she could go without water is roughly three days. Guessing it's been about sixteen to twenty hours since she last ate or drank anything (breakfast before the boat trip), Cally decides she has about two days before she needs water. She has about a week before she will die of starvation, so she sets food and water aside for the time being.

It could be argued that she needs to start looking for resources now, but her current state could lead her to waste more calories and become more fatigued than if she were to wait a day.

She looks at her surroundings, her gaze settling on the rocky ground. I could make the space more comfortable... she ponders to herself.

Deciding to move her body as little as possible, as to not waste her precious calories or risk injuring herself more, Cally sits herself back down against the wall. Little by little, she picks up the rocks and tosses them aside.

She slowly clears the area of rocks, leaving just sandy, pebbly ground. This way, she won't bruise herself on the uneven ground when she sleeps. Scooting herself forward, she continues, all the way to the water, which is much farther away than it was yesterday.

This is probably due to the tide, she realizes. It was probably high tide when she feel asleep, and low tide now. The low tide has given her access to at least fifteen more feet, doubling her earlier guess in size.

After some consideration, Cally has arranged her little beach almost as if it were her home. It is a silly idea, really, but it helps her cope. Adding at least some sort of normalcy helps her to adjust with the reality that she might not survive. She can at least be comfortable while she withers away, right?

The area against the wall where her tank top is laid as a mini blanket will serve as her bed. The place to the left of the mini bed, behind a large rock that is quite close to the water's edge will serve as her bathroom. When the tide comes up, it will wash away any excrement. On the other side is her sink; a little puddle. She realizes that her little 'sink' is rather unreasonable and in no way sanitary, but it's the thought that counts.

She hadn't decided on any other rooms, but she does feel like the right wall with all the pockets from years of erosion would be a perfect place for a book shelf. A potential library, maybe? She ignores the fact that she has no books.

However small it may be, Cally smiles.

Cally whimpers, her hand gently holding her gurgling stomach. It's been many hours since she awoke, probably six to eight at least, though she has no way to be certain. The sun has set, the waning moon reflecting on the ocean's surface and into her cave. The rippling water reflects the light onto the cave's ceiling, bathing the cave in a dull glow.

Another whimper slips past Cally's lips as she becomes light headed. She rests her head back on the wall behind her. Hunger is a lot harder to overcome than she had originally thought.

About two hours after she awoke, she began to get dizzy. Three hours after that had her pale and her vision swimming. Ever since, she has been slumped against the wall, her body too weak to do anything else. Not that there is anything for her to do, anyways. Go to the bathroom, maybe. But after already going twice, she isn't sure there is much left for her body to expel.

Not only is Cally hungry, but she is also in so much pain it nearly has tears running down her face. The day's exercise combined with the lack of sanitation has her entire body stinging. The blood and ooze has since dried, therefore any movement causes the scabs to crack and pull at her skin.

The very centers of the cuts are covered in milky green puss, a grotesque sight to her innocent eyes. Her own nose crinkles in disgust as she peers at the disgusting flesh. She has also noticed that the laceration on her thigh does not go straight in, but at an angle, causing the flesh on the inner side to pull up of she pries at it.

On the bright side, her broken fingers are not crooked, which means they should grow back straight as long as she doesn't mess with them while they heal.

Cally briefly wonders how long it will take for the rumored 'hunger pains' to set in. Is it two days? Three days? It doesn't matter, really. Cally isn't sure how much more pain she can endure.

She should wash her cuts, right? The salt water should clean them a little bit, right? At this point, Cally needs a distraction to take her mind off the hunger nawing at her empty stomach.

With gentle yet shaky movements, Cally slowly drags herself to the water's edge. The tide has since gone up, giving her about a twenty foot gap between her and the water. Twenty feet has never seemed farther for Cally.

She has now mastered the art of sliding herself backwards and forward in her crouched position. It is in no way easy or painless, but it works. She is able to move much more efficiently and much faster than when she first started.

Finally at the water's edge, Cally dips her feet in the dark waters. The sea feels warm compared to the cool air of the cave. The indirect breeze that swirls in the cave gently moves her hair around her face and tickles her neck. She had tied it into a bun as best she could, but it still sags a bit. The injuries on her stomach and ribs make raising her arms quite difficult.

And so she sets about cleansing herself in the ocean's salty water. Extremity by extremity, she removes the grime and sand from her body. She gently hums, her breath hitching in pain every so often, but the gentle lull of familiar songs eases her mind.

She is so focused on her cleaning, that she doesn't notice the water rippling as a lithe creature breaks the surface of the stillness. In fact, she doesn't notice him for quite some time. Cally only realizes his presence when he is close enough for her to hear his breathing.

Her head raises slowly, eyes widening and hands stilling as she meets his familiar, unwelcoming dark gaze.

Cally gasps breathlessly and begins to scramble backwards, but her body fails her. She collapses halfway out of the water, her elbows meeting the rough ground harshly and she groans.

The creature watches her struggle. He had smelled her the second she entered the water and was curious to know why she would do such a thing as to enter his domain. His steady gaze doesn't miss the trickle of blood that drips down her leg, its deep red color contrasting against her pale skin.

Cold fear latches its talons around Cally's spine, her breaths shortening into quick pants. Her body aches in protest as she collapses moves slowly back onto dry land, her ankles just out of the dark water. She isn't sure if it's exhaustion or fear that has her unable to retreat further.

Through the semi-darkness, Cally is able to make out the creature's features. His body is only visible from the chest up, the dark waters obscuring his massive tail. His skin is the palest she has ever seen.

Arteries criss-cross over the entire expanse of his skin, the lack of melanin making his epidermis nearly translucent. His dark hair lays over his head in a lazy mop, the top ruffled almost as if he had brushed it out of his eyes upon surfacing. A shiver runs down her spine as her gaze settles on the strange slits on the side of his neck.

His features are sharp and exotic, but hauntingly human. His eyes are the only things to give away his true identity.

Terrifying, obsidian eyes.

There is no difference between pupil and iris. The deep, bottomless pits so full of darkness and death, yet so alive at the same time. The moonlight reflects off of his colorless irises, the shine giving them an ethereal glow of inhuman beauty.

He watches her emotionlessly, his head tilted slightly to the side. Cally wonders if he has come back to finish her off, but if he has, what is he waiting for? Does he not realize that he could easily reach her once the tide comes up? There is no hint of malice in his colorless gaze, only mild curiosity, if that.

The creature glides forward.

"Pl-please, n-no," Cally chokes as she struggles to withhold her tears. She pulls her feet up and curls into a ball on her side, her ribs aching painfully in her abdomen.

The creature slows, his eyebrows furrowing at the human before him. Cally watches with baited breath for the creature's next move. Her eyes widen as he sinks back into the water, vanishing from sight.

She waits a few more beats before she finally lets her muscles relax and her breaths to slow. She watches the spot where he disappeared for how long, she isn't sure. Her eyes seem glued to the area, unable to move from where the frightening creature had been just a few moments ago.

A scream bursts from her dry throat as the creature once again rises back from the depths. Water drips down his pale skin, little droplets dripping from his pointed nose. His tail flicks up from beneath the water, creating a small splash as he propels himself forward.

Cally silently pleads for her life as the creature draws closer and closer. Her eyes widen as he stops merely six feet away. The shallowness of the water has him on his belly, his obsidian tail stretched out behind him.

Cally shivers under his penetrating gaze.

Cally flinches, covering her eyes as he raises his hand, almost as if he were to strike her. She jumps when something slaps on the ground in front of her. Slowly, eyelid by eyelid, she peeks her eyes open. On the ground before her is a small fish about the length of her hand. Her eyes glance out at the water, only to see the creature is nowhere to be found.

Her gaze settles on the dead fish, its head clearly smashed. With trembling hands, she picks it up. She had no way to cook it, and she isn't sure why the creature brought it to her. After many moments of gazing at the small fish, her hunger takes over her.

With a scrunched nose and teary eyes, she sinks her teeth into the raw fish.

# Chapter 6

-------------------------------------------------------

The policeman sighs, pinching the bridge of his nose as he continues the trying task of consoling the grieving family before him.

"I am sorry, but there is nothing we can do at this point," he says, bringing his hands down and clasping them in front of him on his desk. "We understand that your daughter has drowned, and we are doing all we can to find her, bu--"

"For the last time, Officer Warren, my daughter did. Not. Drown." The woman before him seethes, tears welling in her eyes. From grief or frustration, he is not sure.

"Ma'am, I am sorry, but what you are telling me simply isn't possible. There is no such thing as a creature half fish, half man."

"Well then how come we saw it with our own eyes?" Her husband says. "That thing clawed up the side of the boat and took my daughter out of my own hands!"

The startling truth is, they aren't the first ones to say this. Warren has, in fact, heard of multiple accounts like this, but there has never been any proof. He remembers looking at the boat the family washed ashore on. There were clear claw marks etched in to the boat's hull. What on earth could have caused that? There is simply no logical explanation.

Officer Warren gulps. There is an explanation, but it is in no way logical--in no way real. His gaze settles on the distraught husband and wife sitting in front of him, before sliding to beyond the glass doors where their son sits cross-legged against the wall.

The little boy's shoulders are slumped, tear stains clear on his pale cheeks. Warren can't imagine what the boy must be going through, having seen his sister drowned right before his very eyes.

Warren looks back at the grieving couple.

"I'll see what I can do."

Cally has decided that she will never eat a raw fish again without first getting rid of the scales. When she ate the first fish, scales got all in her mouth and were almost crunchy and hard to spit out.

That was two days ago.

Once a day for the last two days, a fish has showed up on the bank. She only saw the creature deliver her food once, the other times she was asleep.

She stares down at the newest fish. Two things about it are different. It is slightly bigger with a black stripe from its tail to its head, and there is a bite taken out of it. Normally this wouldn't deter her from eating it, but she is practically sick with thirst.

She lays the fish aside, the thought of water making her dry throat ache even more. She is happy for the food, yes, but what is food without drink? She was even so desperate for water that she tried licking the water off the cave's walls. It was salty.

The part of her brain that isn't thinking about water, is wondering why the creature is feeding her. Does it see her as a pet? Is that why it took her? If that's true, then it's doing a terrible job of taking care of her.

Cally is broken from her reverie by the creature breaking the surface once more. It is day time right now and not a cloud in the sky, allowing Cally to see more clearly than usual. She is settled with her back against the wall on her 'bed.' She is safe from this distance, but it doesn't stop her from feeling uneasy.

The creature glances at the discarded fish. And, completely catching her off guard, speaks.

"Eat, korítsi," he demands.

Cally opens and closes her mouth like a fish, too stunned to react. His voice is deep and piercing with an underlying hiss to his tone. Of all the things she would have expected him to do, this was not on the list.

"I-I," she struggles. What does she say? What does korítsi even mean?

The creature swims closer.

"Eat."

"I'm th-thirsty," she says shakily. Who is she kidding? The thing could get angry at her for making a request. Who is she to demand anything? He is clearly the one who holds the power here. I'm so stupid, she says to herself.

The creature tilts his head curiously. almost as though he did not understand. He regards her with contempt.

"Eat," He demands again.

"I'm sorry. I-I can't. I'll be sick," she nearly whispers, took scared to speak any louder.

The creature turns away, hissing.

"Why?" He asks with a loud voice, causing her to tremble slightly.

"I need f-fluids. Water, juicy fruit--anything," she says, her need for water overpowering her fear to speak.

The creature snaps his head back around to her, giving her body a once over, before diving back into the dark blue depths. Cally lets out a shaky sigh, glad he has left, but worried she may have made her situation worse.

A few hours later, Cally finds herself staring out of the mouth of the cave. She has gotten better at moving around lately, now able to walk a few steps at a time. Her hip feels much better and most of the bruises are starting to dull. The only injuries not getting better are the cuts on her abdomen and thigh.

Cally sees him coming before he breaks the water's surface. The light from outside allows her to be able to see into the clear water. His tail gently propels him under the surface, his arms still by his sides. Even in a relaxed state, his speed is astounding. He has crossed from the cave's entrance, all the way to the water's edge in just a few seconds.

Cally steels herself for the upcoming encounter with the strange sea creature.

His head rises up, followed by a hand that sweeps his hair to the side. The tide is farthest out right now, and after going down to the edge earlier, Cally knows the floor drops off at that point, becoming very deep in just a few feet.

The creature settles his elbows against the edge, eyeing her from the water. Cally watches as he raises one slightly webbed hand, a pineapple held in his grasp. She gasps at the sight, her body shuffling forward on it's own accord, eager to get a taste of the fruit's tantalizing fluids.

Recognition of her actions have her stopping just feet from the creature. She eyes the fruit hungrily, but is too afraid to take it from him. Her mouth would probably be watering if she had enough fluids in her dry throat to do so. She waits impatiently for him to toss it on shore for her to take.

He slowly sets the fruit on the shore, but he doesn't stop there. His obsidian gaze captures her own as he settles a small, sharp stone next to the pineapple. He keeps his steady gaze locked with hers as he moves back a few feet.

Without waiting any longer, Cally rushes forwards, taking the pineapple and stone. She faintly notices a sting in her hand from the sharp rock cutting in to her palm, but she ignores it. Once more safely away, she wastes no time in using the rock to jaggedly cut open the fruit. Once open far enough, Cally sinks her teeth into the yellow insides, sucking up the juice greedily.

After many minutes of basically attacking the poor fruit like a rabid dog, Cally glances back at the water, only to once again meet the captivating gaze of the creature. She wonders why he is still there. Usually, he leaves just as soon as he came, yet this time he stayed. Cally observes him silently, suddenly very aware of the unattractive mess covering her face from the pineapple juice.

He scrutinizes her carefully, almost as if trying to decipher something, though she can't figure out what. Cally wipes her cheeks and mouth, embarrassed.

"Thank you," Cally mutters quietly.

Shock briefly crosses the creature's face before it is quickly covered by indifference. He eyes the wounds on her leg and stomach, knowing they are not healing well. Without giving her another glance, he dives back under the water.

Even though she might not realize it, the human won't survive long in this state.

# Chapter 7

The creature begins his ascent from the ocean's floor, the medicinal seaweed held loosly in his hand. If he wants the human girl to survive, it seems he will have to do a bit of work.

Aside from being vile, vicious creatures, he also realizes humans are very needy. He knew the human would need food to survive, so he provided it. But what else did she need? Water, she had said. Fruit...anything. His kind did not require such things.

Such puny creatures. They couldn't even drink from the ocean! It was indeed water, last time he checked. And so he set about tending to her needs, all the while wondering why he didn't kill her when he had the chance.

He isn't sure why he didn't eat her. Yes, eat her, as that's what his kind tend to do to the humans. He had been watching her from the water for quite some time before the storm. One could say he was stalking her. And indeed he was, with every intention of tasting her human flesh. It was only what she deserved, afterall.

Humans are quite the delicacy among his kind. He had only tasted one human before. He did not regret tearing into the human's flesh with his teeth while it was still alive and screaming. The foul creature deserved everything it got.

And yet, he still did not kill the girl. Why? He is not sure. She was innocent, kind, caring, everything he wanted for the purpose she was to serve, and yet he couldn't go on with his plan.

When he took her that day during the storm, he thought it was to devour her like he did the man, but he couldn't. Once he held her fragile body in his arms--once her legs had ceased their kicking--her lungs filled with water, he found himself incapable of harming her. No, he had tried to tell himself. Humans are foul, vile, disgusting! And yet, he could not make his claws sink into her flesh.

Instead, he found himself swimming to the surface, holding her limp body above the water. He then took her back to the cave she is in now. There, he practically squeezed the water out of her lungs, nearly forcing life back into her body.

And there he left her. He didn't think she would survive, but life can surprise us sometimes. She was a little more beat up by the storm than he had originally thought, and to top it off, her wounds became infected. Humans... So weak.

He breaches the surface, his breathing patterns switching from his gills to his nose. He swims towards the cave, the seaweed still in his grasp. It is a medicinal weed that is only found on the far edges of the reef. His kind has used its healing powers for centuries, his mother had told him. He wonders if it will work on the human.

It is high tide now, making her sleeping form accessible from the water. He might have to slither forwards on his belly a few feet to reach her, but he will manage that with ease.

As the water shallows, he pulls himself with his hands, careful not to make too much sound that would awaken the sleeping girl. Once as far as he can go, he tosses the seaweed onto the bank before dragging himself onto the sand. Subconsciously, he is glad that she removed all the sharp stones.

He rests himself on his elbows, his upper body hovering over her sleeping form. He watches her curiously. His kind do not sleep--well, they can--but that's only during specific times.

He watches as her chest rises and falls, shuddering on the exhales. Her brow is slightly furrowed, showing that she is, indeed, in pain. The girl's face is pale, her lips a purple-blue color. He takes a moment to glance over the strange coverings on her body.

She wears a tight, blue strappy material over her chest and a thicker, more worn looking material covers her waist. He is not sure why she covers her breasts like she does; the females of his kind do not wear such coverings.

Deciding he wouldn't stare any longer, he begins his work wrapping her wounds with the weed. He really does not know why he is doing this. Maybe he might feel bad about purposely crashing her boat, but then again, maybe not. Maybe subconsciously he wishes to make his food more healthy before he consumes it.

Yes, that is more likely.

Cally is awoken by something wet and sticky wrapping around her leg. She whimpers as something painfully jabs into her thigh, right over the laceration. Startled, her eyes fly open. He looms over her, a passive expression on his face.

A scream locks in her throat and she finds herself frozen, unable to flee.

"Don't," he warns her sternly.

Despite his warning, she begins to struggle, her arms raising to push him away from her. Cally screams, only to be cut off by one of his massive hands clamping over her mouth. He easily catches her wrists with his other hand and pins them to her chest. The added weight on her lungs causes her to wheeze and her ribs to grind painfully against each other.

"I said don't, ilíthio korítsi."

Cally looks up at him with fear in her eyes. Is he finally about to finish her off? If so, what is he waiting for? Clearly her strength is no match for his.

"Stop it while I fix you. One move, and I might just kill you," he says, grumbling other words under his breath in another language. Cally ceases all movements.

She watches as the creature lay awkwardly on its side, his long, black tail stretched out beside him and curled slightly. Slowly, he lets her hands and mouth free, eyeing her with a warning look. He reaches beside him and picks up a long, slimy black weed from the sand.

It jiggles and leaves a dark colored slime in its wake, its foul smell permeating the air around them. The creature lays it on her thigh carelessly, Cally only jerking slightly, too afraid to move.

She breaths harshly through her nose and squeezes her eyes shut, white hot pain running through her body like lightning as the creature uses the slimy weed to scrape inside of the cut. His clawed fingertips gently scrape the puss out of the laceration before stuffing the weed inside.

He then moves onto the lacerations on her arms, performing the same procedure. Cally remains still the entire time, nearly blacking out from the pain a few times. Only the stifled moans slipping past her lips and the way her fists clench and eyes squeeze shut show how much pain she is in.

The creature was quite surprised by the human's resilience. He had expected her to writhe and squirm throughout the process, but she remained calm and still, for the most part. He did notice that she did not like his hands on her abdomen. He couldn't blame her, though, with his claws so close to her life sustaining organs.

He wouldn't have actually killed her if she moved, but then again, he might have. His last meal consisted of a small fish he caught about eight hours ago. It was about time he ate again.

With all of the cuts sealed with the weed, she would need to remain still for a while whilst the weed disinfected the wounds. Then he would remove what was stuffed inside and wrap it around the outside like a bandage.

He leans back to admire his work. He had only ever done this to himself when he had had altercations with others of his kind or sharks. His kind didn't exactly get along with each other. They were known to be rather territorial creatures.

The seaweed isn't stuffed in quite as far as it should be on her abdomen, but it will do. The girl's breaths are shallow and he can hear her heartbeat slowly thumping. Her eyes are closed and her muscles relaxed. She must have passed out at some point. There is no way she would trust him enough to fall asleep in his presence.

He would leave her here, but she bled onto the sand and he can't have the scent of fresh human blood attracting any of his kind. With that thought in mind, he rolls over onto his back and stares up at the roof of the cave. As long as he stays, his scent will ward off any other predators.

He can't have something else taking his catch.

# Chapter 8

It's been five days since the creature wrapped her wounds with the seaweed. Five days, adding up to nearly more than a week spent in the cave. Five days without any progress towards returning home. Five days of grief for her family. To Cally, it feels like five weeks.

Her days have been rather monotonous, consisting of a repetitive schedule that grows less appealing each hour, not that it was even appealing to begin with.

First, she eats the fish that is delivered while she sleeps. Second, she walks about her makeshift home to test her strength and massage her joints. Third, she waits for the creature to return with fruit. Sometimes he does, sometimes he doesn't. Lastly, she uses her 'bathroom' before laying down against the back of the cave to sleep.

And then repeat.

She is surprised by how easily she has gotten used to eating the raw fish. She would normally throw up at the thought, but lately, she has been so hungry she nearly craves her daily fish with only being fed once a day.

She is a bit more comfortable with the creature than she first was. His occasional presence with fruit at midday doesn't startle her as much as it used to. Yes, she is still too afraid to speak to him, but she doesn't tremble and shake whenever he is near. He brings her food and doesn't attack her while she sleeps, surely that means he has no current intent to harm her, right?

She thinks back to when he put the healing seaweed on her wounds. That night's events caused many questions to manifest in her mind, one specific one bouncing around her head, forcing itself to be acknowledged. Why did he help me?

Sure, she was in a terrible state, but he was the one who put her in that state to begin with. His expression gave away no indication as to what might have been running through his mind. His eyebrows remained furrowed and his jaw set. She finds his behavior quite intriguing, yet all together beguiling.

Another question is who is he? Or better yet, what is he? Yes, she has seen documentaries and fairytales about mermaids. But she would not call him that, no. Monster or flesh eating sea creature describe him more accurately. He is definitely not some peaceful little mermaid looking for love. He looks more like a blood-sucking, flesh eating, bone crushing, serial killing, kidnapping monster.

She only wishes she had the guts to question him.

Its nearing dusk now, and a storm has been brewing, dark blue clouds assembling along the horizon. It doesn't seem as severe as the storm that her family was caught in, but it is certainly no passing shower. She calmly watches the clouds roll in and assemble as it grows, like an army preparing for battle.

Cally sighs. It is very silent in the cave, the only sounds being the ocean waves outside her little home, and the sound of her breathing. The creature never speaks, unless it's a one word command, and she is too afraid to talk to him. A part of her wishes he would speak more. What would he say? What is he like? She can think of loads of things she would ask him, but at the same time her fear still holds her mouth shut. Perhaps staying quiet is safer anyways.

She rests her back on the wall. How she wishes something--anything--would fill the deafening silence. The immense loneliness eating away at her conscious left her begging for any sort of companionship. At this point, screw fear! She would talk to the creature, if only he were actually around. But maybe there is something she could do about that...

"Cre--" her voice cracks from not having spoken in so long. "Creature?"

Creature is the name she has given him in her head, as she has no idea what his real name is, if he even has one. Is the name offensive? Probably, but it's too late to take the name back now.

"Creature?"

Silence.

"Please, I just wanted to... talk?" She facepalms. Wanted to talk? What a stupid thing to say. Why would he want to talk to her? He doesn't seem like the type to chit chat. Perhaps she is more desperate than she had originally thought.

More silence.

"Ugh!" Cally frustratedly throws a rock into the water. He probably isn't even there. Who is she kidding? Of course he isn't. He probably couldn't even hear her from below the surface. She is trapped, utterly alone, with a mythological creature. She cannot escape until she is healed, which is taking forever. That, and how could anyone find her in a place like this? She is in a cave without an exit. How much more trapped and hopeless can a person feel? Her ribs hurt, her head hurts, her stomach is constantly grumbling, and on top of that, she still doesn't even know if her family is safe. Add to it the fact that she hasn't seen the sun in days, which can't possibly be healthy.

Tears prick Cally's eyes. It has been days since she last cried, but it seems the tears are back. She looks out over the dark waters that act so much like a prison. She wouldn't wish this upon anyone. Complete and utter hopelessness crashes over Cally like a tsunami. Cries of frustration and grief escape her throat in bitter sobs.

Her fear and exhaustion seemed almost dormant until now. Her lower lip wobbles as she shakily raises a hand to swipe the tears from her eyes. Oh, what she wouldn't give just to see her family one last time. Were they thinking of her now just as she had been thinking of them? Were they worried for her, and were they scared? She hoped not. As comforting as it is to know people cared for her, she doesn't want them to feel the pain of her loss.

"Why did this happen to me?" She asks aloud. Her own question echoes back at her. Why did it have to be her? Why did it have to be the girl who had a little brother to get back to?

Oh, Ethan...

She remembers the song she used to sing to him the most. It was her favorite to perform for him, and he loved it just as much. She's sang it countless times. Maybe singing it once more wouldn't hurt? Even if he weren't here to hear it? Would singing it now without him feel the same as it did before when they were happy?

Through her sniffles, Cally begins the song, the lines slowly going from words choked by sobs, to notes sung with elegance.

Titus was BornUnder the eye of a stormRainwater carried his bedAround the world and back againOh, all the things he did seeLife is a dreamDrifting at sealt's so hard to believe

With the first verse over, she looks around the cave, its rocky walls staring back at her. She closes her eyes. If she could imagine the instruments were playing with her, she could imagine she were somewhere else.

And so, Titus would growTall and strong as an oakRainwater stuck in his headIt filled him with words left unsaidOf all the things he might beDrifting at seaAt night he would dreamOf old storms at bayTo wash the pain awayRains fallingFalling on you

Cally's voice filled the silence of the cave with sweet, melodic notes of rainy nostalgia. She imagines she was back at the bungalow on San Mahina, Ethan humming along with her. Cally's head nods to an imaginary beat, her fingers tapping to the silent strum of a guitar. She doesn't have to hear the music, she can feel it. Her tears have long since dried.

And the storm, it was drivingWashing awayAll the trees on the island

Rainwater, rainwater

In the eye there was a silenceBut he washed it awayCrashing rocks by the sirens

Its falling on you

And so Cally continues the rest of her song, the very wind singing along with her.

She was unaware of the creature in the water not twenty feet away, his back resting against a boulder, blocking him from view. He heard her every word, his entire being held captive by her voice. He had never heard anything so beautiful. And indeed he did hear all of it, every note, every line--everything--even her soft cries and choked sobs.

For he came at her first call.

# Chapter 9

------------------------------------------------

Cally is awoken by a cool moisture lapping against her feet. She shivers, pulling her knees up towards her chest. She falls back asleep, shielding her ears from the thunder outside.

Once more she is awoken, this time by something splashing against her back, soaking her bare skin. Cally jolts into a sitting position, temporarily forgetting her injuries as the shock forces her awake.

She blinks her eyes open, only wishing she hadn't a moment later. The traumatic sight before her is one that reminds her all too well of the night she was taken. Thunder booms and lightning crackles across the night sky. The waves surge into the cave, splashing over the rocks and against the cave's walls with deadly force.

Cally scrambles back against the wall, the water rising higher and higher towards her.

Her small patch of land that was once plenty large enough to move around on is now a fraction of that size. Only her little bef is out of the water, the rest having been completely covered by the rising tide. Cold fear travels up Cally's spine as flashbacks of the storm that nearly took her life replay in her head.

Water.

Choking.

Screaming.

Pain.

Cally scrunches up against the wall, her body folding in on itself as fear wraps around her like a constricting snake. Whimpers escape her lips as she tries desperately to block the images from her mind--images that are becoming all too real again.

Her once deep breaths become useless pants as panic settles in. She squeezes her eyes shut and balls her hands into fists. Not again, not again, not again!

Her chest aches as she fails to take deep breaths, her head throbbing and her body feeling as if the very walls were holding her down and trapping her in a hell of their own. She might be able to swim if the water were calm, but not in this--no--not in this. She would die, impaled on the rocks, long before she made it to the cave's mouth, let alone into the storm.

The water steadily rises, the cool seawater lapping against her back and submerging her ankles. There is no dry land now. A scream escapes her lips as a bolt of lightning crackles through the night, the flash alighting the horror scene before her.

Up the waters rise, like demons reaching to grab her and take her into their haunted depths. Cally's entire body shakes and shivers, her breathing erratic and heart thumping wildly in her chest. Her nails dig into the stone wall, her forehead resting against the wet stone.

A giant splash washes over her, soaking Cally all the way to the bones. Broken sobs choke forth from her heaving chest as fear and despair take over. The dark sea nearly has her now. It will take her under--swallow her whole.

A shrill scream tears through her throat as a vice-like grip clamps over her upper arm. Cally is helpless as she is torn away from the wall, her body being dragged into the raging sea. She is roughly turned around only to come face-to-face with the creature with his haunting dark eyes.

Cally kicks her arms and legs, struggling to distance herself from the creature, yet also trying to keep herself afloat. She splutters and chokes as water sloshes into her mouth.

The creature tugs her firmly against his chest, careful to keep her head above the water's surface. The girl only kicks more.

"Stop fighting me!" He shouts over the wind and storm. "I'm trying to help you!"

Cally freezes. That thought hadn't occurred to her yet, as she had been solely focused on freeing herself from his grasp--on surviving. As another wave splashes over them, she grasps his shoulders in an effort to stay above the surface. She is surprised at the amount of waves inside the cave. She pales at what may lay outside the cave's protective walls.

"Let me know when you need air," is all he says before covering her mouth with his webbed hand and diving under the raging waves.

Cally is instantly plunged into darkness. She grasps desperately to the creature's shoulders as they dive deeper and deeper. The water soon becomes fridgidly cold and Cally feels her ears popping. Soon, her lungs start to burn with the lack of air, the aching force of lost oxygen filling her chest like fire.

Cally starts to struggle in the creature's grip, her fist banging on his shoulder. Recognizing her silent plea for air, he redirects their path, heading straight for the surface. Cally's ears pop once more just before they reach the open air.

Cally gasps for air as soon as her mouth is free of the creature's hand. She gulps in greedily, chest heaving beneath the tight hold of the creature's arms. Her vision blurs and her head feels as though it is being compressed by a vice, probably due to the pressure changes underwater.

The creature holds the girl tighter and he feels her body starting to become limp. What's wrong now? He has done everything needed to keep her alive, even rescuing her from drowning in the tide, and now she decides to die?

The creature yanks her hair back to raise her head from falling into the water. She winces, which is good. It means she isn't dead yet. An uncomfortable feeling stirs in the creature's chest at the thought of her being dead.

"Wake up, korítsi!" He gently slaps the girl's face. Her eyelids slowly flutter open and she nods her head once.

"See the land? I will get you as close to the beach as I can." Cally follows the creature's gaze to a strip of sand just visible through the darkness. She begins to shake her head. The waves that crash there... She will never make it.

"Do you understand?" He demands.

"B-bu--"

The creature dives back under the water before she can finish. The same process of diving down and swimming up is repeated, Cally's head aching relentlessly and unconsciousness looming closer.

The creature guides them through the breaks in the waves, surfacing and diving below the colliding currents. He drags her beneath his arm as he forces them to shallow ground. The creature sinks beneath a crashing wave before resurfacing again, turning the girl to face the beach.

"Go!" He screams in her face. "Go now or you won't make it!" The swell of another large wave curls closer and closer, Cally's shaking body beginning to swim of it's own accord as she races away from it.

The slow pull of the curren grips around her legs and drags her backwards, the girl losing her footing and becoming dead weight as the current sweeps her away. The large wave crashes over her with the force of a freight truck, slamming down on her shoulders and flipping her over and over and over again.

Her feet kick sand, her back dragging across the bottom before she is flipped again to land on her stomach. Her adrenaline filled veins force her arms into action, pushing her body up again. The beach... She made it.

Cally stumbles forward, small waves crashing against the backs of her legs, making her nearly fall once more, but she pushes forward. She clambers up the sand, harsh coughs spluttering from her throat. Her chest burns and her head pounds, skin raw from colliding with the rough sand.

Once finally on the shore, the rain continues to pelt down on her, her hair plastering to her forehead. She collapses on the shore, her body aching from exhaustion, the adrenaline slowly leaving her body.

Amidst the torrential downpour, Cally loses consciousness, her body laid on the sand exposed to the raging storm.

The creature watches from the water as the girl becomes motionless.

He wonders if she just lost consciousness, or if she really did die this time. She didn't take too well to being under water. Why do humans have to be so fragile? All of that work, just for her to die again? He could have just left her for dead, but that would be a waste, wouldn't it?

He angrily dives back beneath the waves, returning to the bottom of the sea where the current is stable.

Why couldn't he have just killed her to begin with? Humans deserve to die--all of them--every last one, so why couldn't he have killed her? He has no doubt that she would have had a delightful flavor, but what was stopping him? He had watched her back on the island for many days, planning his attack.

She was exactly what he needed for his purpose. Sure, there were many others he could have killed, but he wanted her. He knew why, but at the same time, finally getting to see her so close, realizing just how real she was, caught him off guard. She moved with grace, and smiled with beauty. Her blonde hair was also new to him, especially her grey eyes and perfect skin.

Maybe that's why she was different. She was blemish-free amongst a race of imperfection, far too similar... It was inconcievable, really, to see something so perfect related to something so vile. Humans are evil, shameful, nasty things, but the girl was not.

The girl was just like her.

# Chapter 10

Cally is awoken by something skittering over her hand. Startled, she jerks her hand back and sits up. Her eyes open just in time to see a little sand crab scurrying back into its hole. Her eyebrows furrow. Her gaze quickly glances around, her eyes darting back and forth over the unfamiliar surroundings.

She lays on a white, sandy beach, the waves rolling onto the shore before her. Fallen palm trees and drift wood surround the area behind her, and a jungle-like forest behind that. The sun beats heavily down upon her skin and she shields her eyes from its blinding rays.

Sun... Sun!

Last night's events come flooding back to her.

She lay passed out on the beach for the entire storm? No wonder she is covered from head to toe in sand. Suddenly, a giddy feeling bubbles in her chest. A smile pulls at her dry, cracked lips and a lazy laugh escapes her scratchy throat.

"I'm finally free," she whispers to herself.

No cave.

No cold nights.

No musty smell.

"I'm finally free!" She repeats, this time louder.

Cally flops down on her back, her arms and legs sprawled out, soaking in the sun. She may still have no idea where she is, but anything is better than that blasted cave.

After many minutes spent laying in the sand, Cally decides to explore. She pulls herself into a sitting position, her sore body aching in some areas, especially the raw areas where the sand gave her burns.

She hobbles to the water. Cally bends down, mindful of her ribs, and splashes water onto herself, removing the sand from her skin. Her ribs still ache painfully, but at least her hip and shoulder joints are no longer swollen and purple.

She happily hums to herself as she continues washing, a lazy smile on her lips. She has found it quite difficult to be happy lately, which is why she finds it so easy to smile now. She is learning to find happiness in the little things.

Her thoughts drift back to the previous night. She can't seem to comprehend the creature's actions. He kidnapped her, only to heal her and then save her life? She can't help but think: is he really a monster?

Maybe she was wrong about him? Maybe he isn't some murderous monster? But then again, why would he attack her in the first place? Cally comes to a conclusion that is rather unfortunate. The only way she will get answers, is if she were to ask the creature himself.

The island is small, Cally discovers. It is only about two or three acres in size and is circular in shape. Most of the island is just long flats of sand, but the very center has a few palms and some exotic looking bushes. Too bad all of the plants are too pokey and sharp to use as bedding or suitable shelter. They should make good tinder though.

She keeps her eyes peeled for a good spot to make a shelter. To her right is the sea, to her left is thick, impassable shrubbery. She slows her pace to a stand still as she finds a peculiar tree. Its trunk leans at an angle out towards the water, its slender branches extending out towards the sea, the ocean's breeze ruffling its leaves.

Two particular branches stretch out parallel to the ground about five feet above the sand. An idea starts to form in her head. She spotted a beat up plastic tarp earlier. She wonders if it would work as a roof if she were to tie it over the two branches.

She quickly turns around and starts heading back up the beach to the tarp. Only a portion rests above the ground, which means she will have to dig the rest up out of the sand. Cally sets about doing just that, her hands eagerly scraping away the sand to free her treasure.

Half an hour and a sunburn later, and Cally has finally freed the tarp from the sand's evil clutches. One would think sand would be easy to dig in, but not when the thing you are trying to dig up is buried four feet under.

She rests back on her haunches, the sweat making the sand stick to her skin uncomfortably. Pulling herself up from the ground, she drags the tarp back to the tree. It ended up being at least fifteen feet long and around twelve feet in width.

By the time she reaches her soon-to-be home, she is panting heavily with sweat dripping out of every pore. She cringes at the thought of how bad she probably smells.

She has been wearing the same clothes for over a week now, and they are definitely worse for wear. No matter how many times she removes the clothes and rinses them, it doesn't do anything to clean them.

She would kill for soap at this point.

She spends about 20 minutes setting up her little camp. She clears out the underbrush and drapes the tarp over the branches. She has dug a hole and pushed the excess sand to the open end of her makeshift tent as the third wall. She fills the hole with some of the firewood she scavenged.

By this point, the sun is already setting. She had planned to use a piece of broken glass she found to reflect light from the sun onto tinder to start a fire, but it appears she will have to wait until tomorrow. She cringes at the thought of having to sleep on the sand. Tomorrow, she plans to find something--anything--to lay on. Be it wood, leaves, or a freaking rock, anything is better than the rough sand, especially since she got a sunburn today and her skin already hurts.

Cally sits at the opening of her tent, waiting patiently. For what, she is not sure, but found the answer when her eyes settled on a pair of obsidian ones.

The creature has been watching the girl for quite some time now, many hours actually. He is surprised by what she was able to accomplish all in one day, but he is more surprised by why he found himself watching her all day. She is quite oblivious, he realizes. She never once noticed his constant stare--never noticed his dark gaze analyzing her every movement.

He would have to keep an eye on her, then. There are many predators like him who would jump at the chance to sink their claws into an unsuspecting human.

They could harm her in other ways too, especially with the Great Tide coming.

He subconsciously swims closer to shore.

The creature watches as she settles herself in the sand at the front of her shelter. She scans the horizon, her grey eyes gazing out at the darkening waters. Too caught up in observing her, he forgets to hide himself. Her eyes land on his, a surprised look settling on her delicate features.

Deciding he'd rather not scare her any more than she already is, he goes to turn away, but is startled to hear little splashes of feet in the water. He turns around to see her knee deep in the calm waters, an anxious expression on her face. He eyes her carefully, waiting for her to make her next move.

Cally has no idea what came over her.

She has no idea why she willingly went into the water, with the creature, and in the dark. This was, by far, one of her less intelligent decisions.

She clenches her fists tightly, willing her nerves to steady. I will not run. He hasn't hurt me, yet...

"Why?" She asks. No context, just why.

"Why, what?" He responds, not really sure what she is asking. There are a lot of things she could be referring to. Why kidnap me? Why haven't you killed me yet? Why am I here? Why--

"Why did you save me?"

Out of all the questions she could have possibly asked, she had to ask the one he did not know the answer to. The creature groans audibly.

"What's it to you?" He growls, an annoyed look settling on his perfectly sculpted face.

Cally, noticing his displeasure, quickly backtracks. "I'm sorry, I-I was ju-just curious," her voice shakes.

The creature closes his eyes and exhales loudly, keeping his temper in check. He forgets how easily he is angered. She was just curious and he couldn't blame her for that, but he also didn't owe her any answers, especially if they were answers he didn't wish to share.

"Thank you," she whispers.

There it is again. That phrase. He remembers the last time she said it, and it had shocked him then, too. His kind do not use that term.

The creature finds himself moving closer to her. She was just so... strange. There were things about her that he struggled to comprehend. Why would she thank him if he was the one to cause her pain to begin with?

Cally stumbles back as the creature suddenly moves closer. His onyx eyes squint slightly as he observes her more closely. Despite having spent so much time in the creature's presence, she still finds herself trembling at his nearness.

"M-my name is Calliope," she whispers, her delicate voice flowing into the creature's ears. He looks into her grey eyes. He once saw another human with grey eyes, but his were cold, lifeless, masking the evil soul which lay behind them.

Hers, however, are rather different.

They are calm and serene. They are like a rain shower brewing in the sky. They are knowledgeable, wise. He can't imagine an evil soul dwelling behind those eyes. They are, dare he say, beautiful. Her eyes remind him of her, not in that they look the same, but that they carry the same caring gaze.

The creature backs away, his lithe form relaxing into the welcoming sea he calls home. The girl, Calliope, remains still in her place, her gaze following him. Before turning away, his deep, commanding voice sounds in her awaiting ears.

"I am Atlas."

# Chapter 11

-----------------------------------------------------------------

Cally's entire body is still as she holds the glass at just the right angle to where the sun's light shines onto the tinder in a piercing ray of flammable light. She must hold it in the exact same spot as to keep the heat in the same place. One little movement, and the heat dissolves, restarting the process.

It has been at least an hour since Cally awoke to her stomach grumbling and her ribs aching. A fish was laid on a rock right on the shore, obviously left for her by Atlas.

Atlas.

It felt strange to call him that. She was so used to calling him creature that any other name seems foreign. She, at one time, wondered if he even had a name.

The fish was still cool to the touch, which meant it could only have been there a few minutes. After scoffing down the raw fish, she decided she had had enough of raw meat. Every time her stomach twisted and her throat gagged.

She had spent three days on this blasted island trying to make a fire, but to no avail. Everything had still been too wet and the air too humid from the storm to make a fire.

She vowed to never eat a raw fish again, and so here she is, her back blistering under the harsh rays of the sun as she desperately tries to light the tinder on fire with a piece of glass.

Suddenly, a small stream of smoke begins to emerge from the dry grass in her hands. Cally nearly jumps up in a happy dance, but quickly stops herself, keeping her body still. She can't afford to mess up now, not after so many days spent trying and failing.

As the smoke grows taller, a tiny flame arises. Slowly, carefully, Cally removes the glass and blows gently, her stiff legs rising to walk to her hut. She carries the precious flame like it's the Holy Grail. Setting it down on a bed of sticks, Cally continues to blow gently.

After a few more minutes of careful blowing and the slow addition of twigs and sticks, Cally has herself a little campfire. An elated laugh bubbles up her throat and Cally throws her head back in a hearty guffaw. Her eyes dance with happiness as she sees her success. Now all she has to do is tend to it and make sure it doesn't go out. Even if it does, though, the coals will be much easier to light next time around.

Cally steps outside her tent as the fire grows too hot. It isn't nearly large enough to burn anything, but with the already warm temperatures, any extra heat is unbearable. Cally coughs, swiping her hand in front of her face as the smoke stirs around her.

Well, this is one task off the list of things she wished to accomplish. Deciding the fire will last without her for a little while, Cally sets about carving one of the larger sticks she found into a spear.

This way, she will hopefully be able to kill her own fish without having to rely on Atlas.

Cally climbs onto a large boulder that rests in the edge of the water near her tent. The water here is deeper, but it gives her a beautiful view of the sea. Future spear and sharp-ish rock in hand, Cally begins to scrape away the outer bark of one end of the stick.

The process is slow and arduous, being that the rock she is using is not the sharpest. She wishes she had the stone Atlas gave her back in the cave. After twenty minutes, only the outermost layer of bark is gone, and the tip isn't even close to being pointy. She takes a break to tend to the fire.

Twenty more minutes, and the rock no longer works well enough to carve away the inner layers. Ten minutes after that, and Cally's arms shake from the effort it takes to even scratch the inner wood with the dull rock.

"Argh!" In a fit of frustration, Cally chunks the rock out into the ocean. She fists her hands in her hair and tosses the stick aside.

"What are you doing?"

Cally jumps and nearly falls of the rock at hearing Atlas' deep voice. Resting a hand on her chest, she slowly calms herself down and takes deep breaths. Atlas cocks an eyebrow, an unimpressed look on his impeccable features.

"I w-was making a spear," she says, her voice small. A dark look casts a shadow over his face, his jaw clenching.

"Why?"

Noticing his rigid stance and angered expression, Cally's expression turns nervous and more than a little frightened.

"It was just so I could fish," she mumbles, subtly sliding backwards.

Suddenly, Atlas pulls himself onto the rock and reaches past her to grasp her half-finished spear. Instead of returning to the water, he stays there, settling himself on his back next to her.

Cally's body goes rigid as he shows no sign of distancing himself from her. His anger seems to dissipate, thankfully, though she remains uncertain as to what angered him so.

Cally's mind fogs as she stares at the creature before her. She had only seen him in the water, never in the open sunlight where she could fully see the extent of his body. She was amazed, yet frightened, at what she saw.

His tail was at least seven or eight feet long, the obsidian scales tinting green in the sunlight. It twitches and flicks occasionally, making Cally jump every time. Scales slowly turn into skin, revealing a prominent V-line between his hips. Lean, defined abs and a heavily muscled chest stare back at her.

Something she also notices, is the scales and small fins on the back of his forearms. She hadn't seen them before. Her gaze flicks back to his chest subconsciously, the multiple scars that litter his skin seem much harsher in the light of day than she had originally thought.

"Why must you fish? Have I not provided you with enough food?" He asks, though it is not with concern, but more like annoyance.

Flustered, she responds: "I--uhm--humans usually eat two or three times a day."

Atlas takes a moment to ponder this. He doesn't understand why humans would require so much food. His kind can go much longer without food than humans can. He had noticed, though, that she wasn't quite as soft looking as she was when he first took her.

"Why?"

At this point, Cally was almost tired of his constant questions, and her mind was still slightly frozen in fear of being so close to him.

"I don't know. It's just how the human body works, I guess."

"This is useless, korítsi," he says, holding up her spear. Feeling embarrassed by her poor craftsmanship, she is quick to defend herself.

"It was the rock," she blames. "It wasn't sharp enough."

"Obviously," he mutters twisting the stick this way and that.

With a sigh, he tosses the stick back into her lap. Humans are so primitive. Atlas drops back into the water, the cool waves enveloping his skin and scales. He welcomes the soothing feeling.

"Stay here," he commands before diving into the cerulean unknown. He has multiple spears of his own, of course, but if she wants something, she will have to work for it herself.

And besides, with the Great Tide coming, she will need a way to defend herself.

Atlas breaks the surface, the harsh sun glaring into his eyes. He never went above the surface before he took the girl, preferring to stay deep in the cool waters on the bottom of the sea. The girl jumps at his sudden arrival, accidentally slipping off the rock and into the ocean below.

The cool water rushes to meet her, her muscles tensing at the sudden change in temperature. She paddles her way back up to the surface, her lungs drinking in a greedy gulp of air. Cally's legs kick to keep herself above the surface as her hands wipe the salty water from her eyes.

Blinking her eyes open, she is surprised by what she sees.

The corners of the creature's lips are tilted up just the slightest bit--just enough to reveal a smile. His eyes shine with something she hasn't seen on him before: amusement. The look is so strange--so foreign--she finds herself wiping her eyes again to make sure she isn't seeing things.

It's beautiful, she realizes. She already knew he was beautiful, but it was that kind of unaproachable beauty, so perfect and flawless it was intimidating. It is almost like he could have been hand sculpted by Michelangelo himself with the finest of marble. He is the kind of beauty others bow down to.

But seeing him like this... It is a different kind of beauty. This beauty is real. It is the beauty that you can touch--feel beneath your fingers--taste on your lips.

For a moment, she forgets the pain he has caused her, and finds herself smiling back at him. Cally almost feels like she has hope--hope that she will find peace amidst the sea of life that is tossing her about so cruelly.

He could easily be mistaken for an angel; one sent to rescue her from this forbidden place, but he is no angel. He is the very demon who put her here.

The spell is broken.

The creature's smile disappears and Cally comes crashing back to reality. His face is wiped clean of emotion, his features hardening into a blank slate clear of any trace of humanity.

Cally turns away, climbing back onto the rock, her safe haven from the creatures of the deep. She clears her throat awkwardly, her eyes cast away from him. She only wishes the moment could have lasted a little longer, if she could have had a little more hope.

"You were doing it wrong, anyways," Atlas says, taking her stick into his hands. He flips the stick around, starting to work on the thicker end. He uses a much sharper stone, one he crafted himself, to shave away the outer bark.

"Always sharpen the thickest end; it throws better this way," he says as he continues shaving away.

Cally nods silently, watching him as he works. Her eyes follow his movements intently, memorizing his technique. It's not everyday that a merman teaches you how to make a spear. Ha! Ethan would find this hilarious.

Cally's features become downcast as she remembers her little brother. She has tried so hard to not think about them and how they must be mourning her loss. If only she could tell them she is alive! No matter how hard she tries to push it away, it seems she can never escape the sorrow she feels.

"Korítsi."

"Human."

"Human!"

Cally jumps at Atlas' sudden shout, as she hasn't noticed him calling her. She is even more surprised when he shoves the stone and the stick into her arms and splashes back into the sea.

"If you aren't going to pay attention, then you can do it yourself," he says harshly, diving under the waves and out of sight before she has a chance to speak.

Feeling coolness on her cheeks, Cally dabs under her eyes with her fingertips.

She hadn't noticed she was crying.

# Chapter 12

-------------------------------------------------------

Atlas has no idea what he is going to do.

He has only hours left--a day if he is lucky.

The Tide is coming, and there is nothing he can do to stop it.

The girl will be in danger, and that is not a complication he can afford. Despite his inability to enact his wrath upon her, the girl is still his responsibility.

Not only that, but it's the kind of danger that has him worried.

He has to get to her soon--before the others. She is defenseless besides her wobbly spear. If only he didn't care! If only he could have gotten rid of her when he had the chance... But now it's too late. Now he...

What is this?

How could he ever accept it, let alone explain it?

Why does the thought of her being in danger bother him so much?

He should leave her for the others. Hell, he should take part of her flesh, himself.

No.

But why not?

What is this feeling that keeps holding him back? Normally, the thought of human flesh makes his fangs tingle with hunger, but the thought of it being her flesh makes him sick to his stomach.

Years past, he would anticipate the Tide, waiting with excitement for the onslaught of females, his nights full of desire and lust, but this year is different. This year, he craves no woman. He only feels the duty to protect.

And then there is the chance of other males sniffing around his human. No doubt they will smell her human scent for miles. No. They will not have her.

She will be his.

Cally sits with her back to the fire, her shadow stretching out before her. There is no moon tonight, the glowing orb completely obscured by clouds. Rain falls from the sky in heavy torrents, little peaks forming in the sand from the splashing raindrops.

Cally is thankful for her tent.

She holds a reed loosely in her hand, its thin bark smooth against her now calloused palms. She uses it to draw marks in the snow white sand--tally marks to be exact.

Twenty-one marks for twenty-one days.

Three marks for three weeks.

Five hundred and four marks for five hundred and four hours.

They are all the same amount of time, but each are told differently. All are equal but differ greatly. All tell how long she has been gone, how long since she has seen the faces of her family members, how long since she heard her brother's laugh, her mother's chiding or her father's words of counsel.

She wonders if she will ever hear Ethan's happy voice again--that high-pitched chuckle full of amusement--see those eyes shining with mirth. Maybe, but probably not. No boats float past on the horizon, no airplanes fly though the air. She has begun to wonder if this island even exists. Maybe this is some sort of imaginary place that only exists in her mind. Perhaps she is back on land, in a coma? It would explain the enigma that is Atlas.

Her calloused hands and blistered feet say otherwise.

This place is all too real to be a dream, an unfortunate truth that brings tears to her already red and puffy eyes. She should be at home right now, on her laptop applying at colleges. She should be going to the movies with friends and enjoying life, but she isn't. She is here.

Half of the hour tally marks have been washed away by the rain, only about two hundred remaining. A small pout forms on her lips; those took forever to draw. The multiplication problems she had made in the sand to count the hours are also gone, but she doesn't mind those being erased by the storm.

Cally shivers, wrapping her arms around herself as a gust of wind blows little rain droplets into her tent. The one good thing to come out of this storm is the drinking water. Last week she had split and whittled out bamboo-like reeds to use as a gutter system to catch water. The water flows into a plastic bucket she found washed up on the beach. It has a hole in the side, so it only fills up about half way, but anything is better than nothing.

Another bonus of the rain is the clean water in general. Before retreating to her tent, she spent about twenty minutes in the rain, just standing there, using it as a shower. Of course, she had no soap, but she did smell much better not having the sweat and sand stuck all over her body.

Literally everything is covered in sand. She has laid leaves on the floor of her tent to keep herself clean of the salty granules, but she has to replace them at least every three days before they become completely trashed. Cally officially hates sand.

A sudden scream has her body flinching.

No, not a scream, an inhuman screech of pain.

It is something she has never heard before. It is like the squeal of a wounded animal mixed with a snake's hiss. The unbearable sound lifts the hairs along her neck, the utterly deplorable sound never ceasing. There is something about a sound so full of pain such as this that triggers the most primal instincts of an animal, be it human or otherwise. The instant, audible trigger of fight or flight was felt so deep in Cally's bones she wondered if it would make her heart beat out of her chest.

It's terrifying.

So much pain and agony in a single cry cannot be good. It makes her wonder what creature could possibly emit such a sound, and doubly what could have frightened it enough to release the horrible scream.

Despite her fear and trembling legs, Cally crawls from her tent, stepping into the cold rain. The dark clouds above completely obscure the moonlight, casting the entire landscape in shadow. Cally can hardly see her own hands in front of her face, much less whatever creature awaits her in the night.

The scream echoes into the night once more, its agonizing howl ripping through the sound of the rain and wind like a knife through canvas. Cally knows she shouldn't have left the tent, but her curiosity and desire to help has her going against her primal need of self preservation.

Her steps are shaky and uncertain, her eyes squinting into the darkness for any hint of her surroundings. The waves slap against the shore on her left, the occasional large one startling her.

Again, the screech, this time closer.

The amount of adrenaline in her veins causes Cally to forget about the coldness of her skin, her brain not even comprehending the rain pelting endlessly on her bare back.

There, she can see it now.

Its body is long, writhing on the sand, grunting and screeching from whatever ails it. Cold fear wraps itself around her spine, chilling Cally to her core. No, she shouldn't be here. She turns to run, her feet digging into the sand as she goes to sprint back to her only safety, but something stops her.

"Human!"

No, it can't be.

She turns around, her eyes widening as she realizes who was the source of the awful screeches.

Atlas lays before her, his body twisting and turning as if he were wrapped in stinging coils. His tail flails about on the beach, fingers fisting in the sand. Low grunts and pants escape his lips as tremors wreak his half human body.

Cally stands motionless, utterly afraid. Up to this point, Atlas was the top of the food chain, but now? Now she wonders who was above him. Whatever hurt him could surely hurt her as well, or worse.

It is not until she begins to watch a little longer that she realizes it is not another creature that has hurt Atlas, rather it was he himself who was causing the pain, whether he could help it or not. As she was frozen on the sand, her eyes glued to him, she realized that he was changing.

His tail, it was shrinking. The blood on his hands was from where he was clawing himself trying to scratch away the scales.

Before she can second guess herself, Cally is rushing to his aid. Her hands go straight for holding his head between her hands to keep him from slamming it against any rocks.

His hands grab at her wrists, his claws slashing against her delicate skin. A cry escapes her lips as blood is drawn. Atlas' obsidian gaze stares up at her, his eyes shining before clenching back shut as another round of pain assaults his body.

He writhes and thrashes and Cally is forced to let him go as he becomes too strong for her to hold. "Please, just stop moving! You are hurting yourself!" She exclaims as his body painfully arches backwards.

She watches in horror as Atlas' claws shrink back into his fingertips, his sickening cries worsening. His scales begin to flake away from his body in a bloody mess on the sand, the fins reshaping to form feet and toes.

One last hiss escapes his lips before morphing into the guttural growl of a man in pain. His fangs visibly shrink into his gum line, blood dribbling down his chin.

Atlas stares back at her once more before his eyes close, his body stilling. What had once been a fearsome creature is now just a man lying in the gory mess of his former nature.

# Chapter 13

---

Cally is dumbfounded by what she has just witnessed. Atlas is no longer a creature, but a man. She sharply turns her gaze away, only catching a glimpse of just how man he really is. Sure, she has seen male anatomy in textbooks and knew roughly what it looked like, but never had she actually seen such things in person.

Ignoring her discomfort, she hesitantly lays her hand against his throat. Beneath her fingers, the tiniest thrum of a pulse is felt. Cally releases a breath slowly from her lips. He is alive, but what to do with him now?

She stares down at his closed eyelids, only just remembering the rain beating down on her back. She can't leave him out here in the rain, but she can't very well let him stay with her? The two of them in her small tent was far too close for her comfort, but did she have any other choice?

Perhaps lending him shelter is her only option besides leaving him in the rain, which is not very kind.

Gritting her teeth, Cally reaches her now bloody hands under his shoulders, and begins to drag him through the sand, back to her hut.

This might not be the correct decision, but it is the kind one. Every few feet, she stops to rest, her back and shoulders aching with the strain of his body weight. She hadn't expected him to be so heavy. Atlas is quite thin and lean, but apparently muscle weighs a lot more than she was expecting.

Soon enough, she has arrived back at her dwindling fire. Atlas is still unconscious in her arms, stoking her worry. She settles him down on a little bed of leaves and sets herself down on the other side of the fire, but not before placing a rather large leaf over his manhood.

Cally spends the next hour or so tending to the fire. Her eyes threaten to close and drift into a much needed sleep, but she forces herself to stay awake. Sleeping would put her in a very vulnerable position were Atlas to awaken whilst she was defenseless.

She is startled by a low groan across from her. Cally stares wide-eyed as Atlas comes to.

Warmth is the first thing Atlas feels when he awakens. His left side is warmer than his right, which is strange. He blearily opens his eyes, only to be blinded by fire, the orange flames making a purple imprint on his closed eyelids.

A low groan sounds deep in his chest as he begins to feel the full affects of his pain. It is always painful after the shift, only, he had forgotten exactly how bad it was. The sudden scent of his human has his gaze snapping up to her's.

Her eyes are wide and alert, her body shrinking into the side of her small hut. He watches her curiously. Last he remembered, he had passed out in the rain. She must have carried him back here. Atlas wonders why she would do such a thing--bringing a monster into her own home.

"Why am I here?" He asks, breaking the silence.

"I-I didn't want to leave you in the rain," she mumbles quietly.

"You should have," is all he says, propping himself up on his elbows. He furrows his brows at the green leaf spread over his middle.

Cally's eyes never stray from him, her grey pools watching him closely for any signs of attack. Atlas can smell her fear easily, it's delicious scent permeating the air around him, mixing with the smoke.

Atlas hisses as he tries to move his sore legs, only for shooting pain to go racing up his joints.

"Are you alright?" Cally hesitantly questions.

Atlas' only answer is to shoot her a glare, to which she cowers back. Part of him likes the idea that she is afraid of him, but the other part recognizes how vulnerable she is to be afraid so easily.

Cally knows she shouldn't be scared anymore, but she can't help it. Sure, he is human--or close enough to it, at least--and he is clearly injured, but she can't help being afraid of her kidnapper.

Atlas removes the leaf from his body, the scratchiness of the foliage not feeling well against his tender new skin. The human girl quickly turns her gaze away from as he does so, causing his brow to quirk at her actions.

"Why won't you look at me?" He asks. "It is never a good idea to turn your back on a predator."

Cally fumbles for an answer, her cheeks heating up at the obvious discomfort of the situation. "I--you," she swallows. "You're naked."

Atlas stretches himself back out on the ground, raising his arms to rest behind his head. "Obviously. Yet I fail to understand why that would cause you to turn away. I am not ugly."

Cally stops herself from agreeing to his statement. Yes, he is definitely far from ugly.

"It is inappropriate to look at someone while they are naked, not to mention an invasion of your privacy," she says quietly.

Atlas hums out a breath, trying to relax his body to ease the pain in his newly acquired legs. His eyelids flutter shut, his long lashes brushing the skin above his cheeks. "Perhaps in your culture, but certainly not in mine. Besides, you can't exactly spend the next month with your eyes closed."

"W-what do you mean, the next month?" Cally questions worriedly.

Atlas rolls his head around to face her questioning gaze. Cally almost flinches at the hungry gaze that lights up his features.

"Why, that's how long I'll be on the island." Atlas pauses then, seeming to ponder over his words. "Of course, if you survive the whole month."

Cally's throat seems to close in on itself, her muscles freezing in their position, eyes locked on the creature lying just across the tent from her.

"I don't understand," she mumbles quietly. She knew this would be coming eventually--knew it was only a matter of time before he finally finished her off.

Atlas was lying.

Of course, he was the only one who knew that, but it did not concern him. He rather liked the cold fright in her expression and the obvious scent of her fear floating in the air around them. The power and control he held over her was immensely exhilarating, a feeling he was used to, and even craved.

"It is a dangerous world out there, my little korítsi. If only you knew how much."

"So, you're going to kill me, then," Cally replies, subtly reaching for the spear that rests behind her.

Atlas frowns dissaprovingly. "No, I never said I would kill you."

That was not a lie. Atlas would not kill her. Had he officially made the decision not to do so? Not to his knowledge, but it had been made, albeit subconsciously.

"But that doesn't mean someone else won't," he continues.

Cally takes a moment to ponder his words. He said he would not killer, but that does not mean he is anywhere near safe or trustworthy.

"Well then, who would?"

Atlas sits up on his elbows then, regarding her blankly. "Are you really so daft as to believe I am the only one of my kind?"

"I just hadn't considered..."

"There are thousands of my kind swarming these waters, all shifting at some point in the coming weeks. They will come to the land looking for females to mate with. In case you hadn't noticed, you are a female, which means you will either be hunted down by other females and killed as competition or you will be taken by the males."

Cally pulls her knees to her chest, her right hand covering her mouth. Her eyes threaten to spring forth tears of fear and desperation as Atlas continues his horrifying explanation.

"Not to mention you are human, which for my kind, is a delicacy," Atlas pauses then, gaging her reaction. "They will still probably make their use of you," his eyes make a cursory glance over her body. "As it would be a shame not to, but human flesh is quite delicious."

"Pl-please stop," Cally stutters. She sniffs back a sob as her eyes betray her, small tears rolling down her thinning cheeks. "I don't want to hear anymore."

Atlas takes in her crying state. It is an unusual sight to him. His kind don't cry, and he hasn't been around humans enough to see them cry. She is the only one he has ever witnessed do such a thing. Usually she cries out of sadness, but this time it is different. Despair. Fear. Apprehension.

He almost wishes he hadn't told the human of what may befall her, but what else was he to do? It was more of a warning than anything. She had to be made aware of the situation somehow.

"You a-abuse your own kind?" She asks, horrified that they could be so cruel.

"Of course not," Atlas sneers. "Our females are more than consenting when it comes to our advances. Only, I don't think you would be quite as keen."

Cally shakes her head rapidly. How could she? Those things behave like animals. Why on earth would she consent to something so feral?

"That's what I thought," Atlas says, watching the disgust shine in her expression.

"So, your people," Cally pauses, fiddling with her fingertips, still uncomfortable looking in his direction, for fear of glimpsing his nakedness. "Their bodies change like yours did, and then what? They just... mate with anyone?"

"You say that with such disbelief, human."

Cally glances up at him then, his gaze pierces into her's, searching the very depths of her soul. "Humans do things very differently," she replies.

Atlas props himself up on one elbow, his other arm resting over his middle.

"Is," she sniffles, drying up the remnants of her tears. "Is there anything I can do to stop it?"

Atlas shrugs.

# Chapter 14

Atlas didn't know his actions were frowned upon. He had lived his entire lifetime observing. He had no intention other than to continue those actions he had practiced so many times before. How should he know staring at someone whilst they slept was uncouth behavior?

He stares at the young woman with renewed interest. Little sounds escaped her lips when she breathed; deep, obnoxious sounds. Yet, in a way, he found amusement in them. The laboured noises could only be likened to a large, rotund man, not the petite little blonde woman.

He almost felt his lips twist up just the slightest.

Her lips are parted, teeth barely visible. Her limbs are still, relaxed more than he has ever seen them. A few strands of blonde hair lay together over the bridge of her nose. He follows the lock of hair with his eyes, down the apple of her cheek, across her jaw, descending the column of her neck, the ends brushing gently against her clavicle.

Her chest rises and falls steadily with each of her heavy breaths, ribs visibly expanding beneath her skin. His eyes don't miss the way her blue clothing has shifted crookedly over her skin. The newly exposed skin reveals a thin line of discolored flesh, or rather, lacking color at all. The new skin is pale, much more pale than the rest of her body, a visible line of darker skin signifying where the blue fabric usually lays

He gingerly reaches a hand forward, fingertips ghosting so lightly across her strangely colored flesh it could have been mistaken for a breeze. Until now, he hadn't noticed she had stopped breathing.

His eyes dart up to lock on her ethereal grey ones. He can clearly see the fear and terror in those silvery orbs. Her chest is completely still below his hand, breath held captive in her lungs.

"Why does your skin look like this?" He asks, dismissing her frightful behavior. He smooths his fingers over the affected area, up over her shoulder.

Cally shudders, limbs stuck as though frozen in ice. She struggles to form words as she watches his fingers move lazily over her skin as though he had a right to do so.

"L-like what?" She whispers, too afraid to make any louder a noise.

"It is two different colors," he answers. "I have seen it before, but I never understood it."

Cally's brows furrow, only just understanding his meaning. "It is called a tan line. Our skin turns darker in the sunlight and, as you can see, the lighter skin has been exposed less, leaving a line."

He tilts his head in interest as he examines her further. "Can I see more?"

Cally blanches. "What?"

"Your 'tan lines' are something my people don't have," he explains. "I would like to see more; they are quite fascinating."

"No," Cally responds in less than a heartbeat.

Atlas frowns, but says nothing more on the matter.

The two are startled by a deep, reverberating sound passing over their heads. The dangerously loud noises pierces their eardrums with distinct force. Atlas flinches, startled by the unusual noise, but Cally has instantly risen, already dashing out onto the beach. She knows that sound all to well.

An airplane.

Only, it is not in the state she would expect. Just as the impending craft passes into view, Cally's mouth drops open in horror. It is a small plane, just big enough to hold a hanfull of passengers. What has Cally stilling in her place, is the thick, black smoke that tumbles out of the engine in endless swirls of doom.

The plane sinks lower and lower, Cally ducking instinctively as it races closer to its ever immanent demise. She doesn't even register her own scream as it crashes nose first straight into the water. The tail and wings rip apart from the frame upon impact, the smaller pieces skidding across the surface before coming to rest and sinking beneath the ocean's surface.

Cally finds herself already waist deep in the water, racing as quickly as she can into the waves to rescue anyone who might still be alive in the ever sinking airplane. She splashes through the water as she desperately begins to swim further away from land. The plane isn't far--only a hundred meters or more. She could make it if she tried.

She screams as a vice-like grip latches around her ankle and jerks her backwards. She whips around, struggling to remain above the surface with her leg held captive.

"What the hell do you think you are doing?!" Atlas spits dangerously.

Cally pays his tone no mind. "Those people. They could be alive!" She gasps, struggling to free herself from him. "I have to save them!"

"You're not saving anyone," he commands. Cally watches in desperation as the plane sinks deeper and deeper. "They are already dead, and if you go any deeper than this, you will be dead too."

Cally's eyes widen as she paddles around to face him. "What do you mean?"

"Did you really not listen to a word I said to you last night?" He admonishes. "That plane will be a feeding frenzy in minutes. If you don't get to shore before then, you are as good as dead."

Cally stares into his eyes--eyes dark as coal--slowly coming to recognition of the situation. She gulps, looking back at the fallen plane, then back at him. Her arms are beginning to tire, the constant paddling wearing on her malnourished muscles.

"Please," her lips wobble as tears spring into her eyes. "Please, we have to help them."

"No."

"Let me go!" She yells.

"No!" He repeats in earnest, adjusting his grip on her leg. She screams and kicks as he begins to drag her back to the awaiting beach. Tears stream down her face as she helplessly watches the plane sink beneath the waves, never to be seen again.

Her heels dig into the soft sand as Atlas carries her up the beach. His arm locks painfully around the lower part of her ribs, the act of inhaling getting increasingly difficult to perform.

He drops her unceremoniously onto the sand, where she remains a small ball with her arms around her knees. Those poor peop le... She could have saved them. What if they had survived the crash? What if the impact hadn't killed them? They--they would have drowned, then. They would have drowned while she struggled helplessly above them.

"How could you be so cruel?" She whispers, but she knows he heard her.

"They didn't survive the landing. The cost of your life would have been an unnecessary sacrifice." His voice is hard, emotionless.

"What if you are wrong?" She asks. "What then?"

She is startled by a harsh grip around her throat, not tight enough to block her airways, but enough to be slightly painful. He jerks her head up sharply to face his. Cally stares up into his eyes as he looms over her, those obsidian eyes wild and crazed as he flashes his teeth at her.

"You mistake me, woman."

Cally whimpers as he rubs his thumb harshly into the column of her neck, his gaze travelling all across her skin with deranged fascination. It would have been a sensual act had his grip not been so tight. He leans closer, his breath hot and invading across her flesh. Cally trembles in fear.

"Yes, I have kept you alive," he whispers against her skin. Cally's chest rises and falls rapidly beneath him. "But I cannot say their fate would have been the same as yours."

He pulls back enough to stare into her eyes again. "Why," he chuckles. "Wouldn't you rather drown," he reaches his other hand up to stroke a finger down the side of her jaw. Cally flinches. "Than be clawed to shreds?"

"St-stop," she whispers.

"I've heard what their screams sound like when you tear their skin from their bones." His gaze draws her in, black pools glowing dangerously.

Cally's tears drip down her cheeks to be caught by his fingers as he brushes them away.

"You wouldn't want that, would you?" He murmurs in her ear, his voice smooth and enticing despite his words. Cally shakes her head as much as she can in his restricting grasp. "That's what I thought!" He whispers harshly, his tone instantly switching to enraged as he shoves her back into the sand.

Cally sobs openly now, her arms wrapped tightly around her as she curls into herself as tightly as possible. She has known fear, yes, but that was new. That was not a kind of fear she was used to.

She doesn't know how much time has passed, but the sun is high in the sky when she finally picks her head up from the sand. Her throat is raw and uncomfortable, aching when she moves it even the slightest.

When she looks around, Atlas' predatory form is no where in sight, and for that, she is thankful.

# Chapter 15

Atlas can hear her crying on the beach behind him. He doesn't regret what he said--not in in the least. The girl was hell-bent on saving those humans even at the cost of her own life. Had she gone any deeper, she would have been found. The others of his kind would have taken her under the surface before she could even scream.

He is in his human body, and he would have been helpless to save her. She just wouldn't listen. She had no thoughts regarding her own safety. If she had been taken... He wouldn't have been able to stop them. Did she not understand that? Was she really so selfless? How could she risk her life for strangers she didn't even know?

She refused to listen to him and he had to make her understand. Atlas wouldn't let this happen again. She needed to know how fragile her life was. He had to make her understand... And he did that the only way he knew how. Of all the time he had spent observing her, he knew one thing for certain: she feared him. The human's fear of him was her fatal flaw--a flaw he could exploit.

He scared her--he had to. Atlas had no other choice but to utilize whatever leverage he had over her. He had to erase any thought of self sacrifice she would have in the future. These waters were deadly, and it seemed he was the only one keeping her from certain death.

Her gentle sobs painfully reach his ears as he wades into the water. Her soft cries feel like knives piercing his eardrums, urging him further away. The human's weeping was something he wasn't used to, as well as something he couldn't handle, especially since he was the one who caused it.

He had felt her trembling beneath his fingertips, her chest as it rose and fell in short pants, how her tears had fallen against his fingertips. She was completely at his mercy and he could have done whatever he wanted with her.

But he hadn't.

He does not understand his actions when it comes to the human girl, so he decides to leave it at that: a mystery. Instead of doing what his instincts and body demanded of him, he left her there, a small, broken girl in the sand. She is better where she is now than in pieces on the ocean floor.

Atlas trudges into the waves, the cool water easily welcoming him home and drowning out the girl's cries. He dives beneath the waves, a part of him feeling as though it were missing as he kicks with his human legs instead of gliding smoothly with the thrust of his tail. He swims further and further beneath the surface, his lungs thankfully able to maintain enough oxygen to keep him from returning.

The others are likely gone by now, as they never stay long. They usually make quick work of the bodies. The water is still relatively shallow by the time he reaches the crash site, shallow enough that the sunlight can still reach the bottom of the sea floor. He pauses his swimming as he looks over the wreckage, toes dragging in the sand. His body relaxes as all the smells of a fresh kill reach his senses.

The scent of blood fills his nostrils, almost catching him odd guard. His head rolls back and his lips part as the high of bloodlust enters his system. He used to love that high, that utterly rabid feeling that would wash over his senses and send him over the edge of sanity. He would lose himself in that feeling of carnal desire for blood and flesh.

Now he only dreads it. He spent weeks suppressing it, every time he was with the human. She would bleed, that crimson liquid rolling down her skin in rivulets of liquid bliss, yet he had to abstain. For whatever reason, he preferred her alive, but at what cost? The cost of his sanity? Until she had healed--with his help, eventually--his life was hell.

Atlas had spent many days just watching her, forcing himself to stay hidden as she would repeatedly rinse her wounds in the water. Her blood would mix and swirl in little pools around her as she scrubbed her skin. The only thing preventing him from caving into his carnal desires was the pain that would etch itself across her face--raw, excruciating pain that would make her lips quiver and tears drip down her pale cheeks.

She was so completely and utterly helpless, much like his mother had been that fateful day. The little human--Cally, as she called herself--was defenseless in every sense of the word. He had taken her that stormy day. He had taken her beneath the waves and held her captive as his very own human object. Just like... Just like...

Atlas' body grows cold as the harsh realization of his actions rises to the forefront of his mind. Is that really what he had done? Were his actions really so similar to those who had taken everything from him?

No, no.

He wasn't--he wasn't like them. This was different. This was payback. She is human--it is what she deserves! Humans are evil. They took everything he loved away from him... But has he not done the same? They had kidnapped his mother and they ki--

No, he was better than that. Maybe the reason he could never hurt the girl was because the situation had been so similar to hers. That... explains everything. Why did he help her when she was starving? Because she was helpless, just like his mother. Why did he save her only a few moments ago? Because Cally cared, just like she did.

Atlas swims down to the wrecked airplane, his appetite for flesh suddenly gone. He would not entertain those thoughts any longer. They were useless to him now. He circles around the crash, observing the various pieces sticking out of the sand. Judging by his past experiences with humans, he knew they always carried personal items with them. Hopefully he could find something useful to him and the girl, presumably still sobbing, back on the island.

Atlas is particularly careful to stay clear of the human remains, not that there is much left of them. He finds the usual knickknacks he always does: cell phones, wallets, cameras, and the like. Inside the plane's hull, it is a complete mess. Atlas pulls his way in, flicking various floating objects out of his way. The cabin groans and shutters as it settles deeper in the sand, but Atlas pays it no mind.

There are a few trunks full of human clothing, though none of them are similar to what the girl wears. Nevertheless, he grabs hold of a particularly large one before making his way back out of the sunken airplane. A few sharks and predatory fish have gathered around the scene at the fresh smell of blood. They circle around Atlas, who ignores them easily. He is much higher on the food chain than them, and they know it.

The trip back to the surface is much longer this time with the added weight of the trunk. When his head finally breaches the surface, he takes in a deep inhale, replenishing his lungs of lost oxygen. Atlas hates his human body.

When he reaches the shore, the water-filled trunk dragging in the sand behind him, the human is no longer in her spot on the sand. He takes this time alone to open the chest and flip through its contents. There are various bottles and containers that he chunks to the side. The clothes and footwear are completely soaked, so he sets them aside to dry in the sun.

He would never usually waste his time with these trivial human things, but he has a feeling a certain human girl would care for them. According to the smell of smoke, she has just started the fire back in the tent, reminding Atlas that she has yet to eat. How he wishes she could go at least three days longer without food like he can.

With a perturbed sigh, he drags the trunk up to the tent, but he does not enter. Instead, he leaves the clothes outside before turning around and heading back down the beach.

He gives one last look at the tent before returning to the ocean, this time for the intent of hunting food for his human.

# Chapter 16

Cally can hear him moving around outside, dragging something large through the sand, but she remains hiding in the tent. She is too afraid to face him right now. The raw fear she had felt was beyond traumatizing. She remembers how angry he had been at her carelessness when it came to her own life. She begins to wonder why he would care so much. The value of her life should have been of no consequence to him. So, why did he feel the need to protect her?

She stokes the fire with a blunt branch, creating spaces for air to reach the center of the flames. She is surprised by how quickly she has picked up the art of fire building. It has proven to be a rather relaxing process, especially for times like this.

It is quiet now outside the tent, so she assumes he has left again. She briefly wonders what he could have been doing out there. It isn't like there is much to do on this island. She still has no idea where he disappeared to after she broke down on the beach. Perhaps he had gone after the plane?

Cally briefly glances in the direction of the fallen airplane. No, she couldn't entertain the thought that they had actually survived the initial crash. If they did, then it was her fault no one saved them.

Content that the fire would survive on it's own for a while, Cally begins to emerge from the tent. She peeks through the flaps carefully, not spotting any sign of Atlas. Instead, there is a large trunk dumped in the sand at her feet. Cally's brows furrow. Did he get this from the plane?

She opens the latch hesitantly, lifting the heavy lid up. She is in utter shock and delight at what she sees. There are clothes, soaps, shoes, a comb, even a small mirror! All of the objects are soaking wet, but this is of no consequence to her. She gingerly carries the clothes to a near by bush, casting them over the branches to dry in the sunlight.

A small pang of sadness seeps it's way into her chest. The owner of these belongings is dead now. A part of Cally knows that using these is wrong, but she can't let the useful items go to waste.

Cally almost cries as she gently holds the bottle of men's shampoo and body wash in her dirty hands. She quickly sets the other things out to dry before making her way to the sea. Perhaps salt water is not the best kind of water to use for washing, but she could care less.

She walks in to where she is ankle deep, the waves lapping gently at her knees. Bending over, she wets her hair, carefully not to get the salty water in her eyes. She squeezes the tiniest bit of soap into her hands, conserving as much of it as possible for future use.

Cally scrubs her scalp like she never has before. She works the shampoo deep into her roots before working her way to the ends. The sharp scent reaches her nose, the pleasant smell more delightful than anything she has ever smelled before. She feels bad rinsing again, knowing the water isn't clean, but it will have to do.

Cally carefully looks around her, spying for any sign of Atlas. When she doesn't see him, she gingerly slips the bikini from her skin. She feels cold and exposed despite being the only one on the island. She makes quick but thorough work of cleaning her body, thankful to finally remove the stench from her skin.

After she is finished, she reluctantly slips the bikini back on before checking to see if the clothes are dry. Feeling the fabric between her fingers, it is still damp, but she will wear it anyways. Anything to be out of this dreaded swimsuit.

She decides on a plain, linen button up for a top and some loose cotton shorts. She removes the swim suit for the last time, setting it aside as she dons the new clothes. The shorts threaten to fall off her hips, but she makes use of some shoe laces that were in the bottom of the trunk to sinch the pants up around her waist.

She rolls up the sleeves of the shirt to bunch around her elbows. The top two buttons she leaves undone, the V of the neck setting perfectly above her chest. Cally decides she rather likes the shirt. It is billowy and cool against her skin. The loose fit is most comfortable compared to the tight straps of her swimsuit.

When she arrives back at the tent, she is surprised to see flames still alight. She had left them quite a while ago and had assumed they would have died out by now. She adds some more pieces of wood, heightening the orange and yellow flames. The smoke dances and curls above the burning wood, tendrils swirling upwards. She watches them intently as the day passes by.

Cally is startled by the sudden presence of Atlas as he slips into the tent on the other side of her. Even more startling is the pair of cargo shorts that sit lowly on his hips. I thought he didn't wear clothes? Cally thought.

A fish is gripped loosely in one hand, a sharp stone in the other. She remains completely still and quiet, observing him with more than a little trepidation as he takes a seat and begins slicing into the fish. He cuts the head clean off, tossing it somewhere outside. He then sliced long ways down the center, remove the entrails and tossing them outside as well. Atlas fillets the fish, scraping away the scales with the dull side of the stone before laying it on a large, flat stone.

Cally is in utter shock at his actions. Never had he done anything like this before. Usually, he isn't even there when he delivers her food, let alone fully prepared it for cooking. She glances up at him, only to see he was already staring at her.

"I-I didn't know you ate your food like that," Cally admits.

"I don't," is his stoic reply. "But you do."

Cally's eyes soften as she gazes at him. Had he done all that for her, then? "Thank you," she softly answers, tucking her chin away from his piercing gaze. She warily eyes his slime covered hands as he grips the stone in his long fingers.

With that, he stands to leave, striding out onto the beach. Without even thinking, Cally rushes to the trunk then trails after him.

Atlas can hear her little feet padding after him through the sand. He rolls his eyes. What could she possibly want from him? He will take care of her as long as she just leaves him alone--

"Wait," she says in a small voice.

He stops, not even turning to look at her as he bends down to reach his hands into the water. He is caught off guard by an object being thrust in his face.

"Here," is all she says, still holding a bottle out in front of him.

He looks up, scrutinizing the girl carefully. "What?" He asks.

"This is soap. You can clean your hands with it."

He raises a brow.

She shuffles a little on her feet, but she remains stoically before him. "You have used it before, haven't you?"

"Why does it matter?" He asks defensively. He does not wish to admit he has no idea what she is talking about.

"Well, it gets rid of the gross stuff on you skin," she explains, understanding that he had no clue what she was on about. "And it smells good."

Atlas snatches the bottle from her, flipping open the cap as he does. He easily recognizes the scent as the one that disgustingly coats her own skin.

"It does not smell good," he says.

"Well, I think it does."

He sends her a glare as he squeezes the tiniest bit onto his fingers before thrusting the bottle back into her hands. It is slick and gloppy between his palms as he smears the soap over his hands. He rinses them in the water, standing back up when he is finished.

Cally wears a tiny smile, her gaze tilted to the ground. She hadn't expected him to actually use it, but he did.

The girl sleeps soundly on the bed of leaves, the fire long since fizzled out. Atlas watches her quietly from the other side of the tent. His fingers toy with the hem of his shorts. Honestly, he has no idea why he wears them, just like how he has no idea why he used the soap she offered.

Perhaps this is another one of those things better left unanswered. He watches her sleep soundly, a black comb still held loosely in her palm. She had spent the longest time trying to remove the knots from her hair, but to no avail. Eventually, she gave up and decided to sleep.

Atlas wishes he could sleep.

Even in his human body, sleep evades him. He does not feel comfortable enough to allow his body rest. Sleep leaves one exposed, and he cannot afford that. Atlas knows it is only a matter of time before the others begin to appear. Anyone could find them while they slept--find Cally.

As his thoughts circle around once more to the girl lying not but a few feet away, he finds himself once again eyeing those blonde curls. They cause her pain.

Cally's hands shake as she tries to pull the comb through the numerous knots that dangle from her head. Atlas observes her as she sits crosslegged by the fire, both arms reaching up to tug at her hair.

Her lower lip is sucked between her teeth, nibbling at the skin as she puts all her focus into the task at hand. She is only working the comb through one small area, yet it still refuses to move. She grips it close to her head with one hand, carefully working the comb through with the other.

Her brow shines with sweat and her eyes are red and puffy. Atlas can tell she is in pain, yet she remains determined.

He had heard her whimpering on occasion, that eventually lead to a sniffle. When she gave up, she curled into a tiny ball, wiping her nose and massaging her head as she did.

Seeing her now, her eyes are no longer red and puffy, her brows smoothed into a relaxed state. Without thinking, he moves gingerly to the other side of the tent. He kneels quietly by her side, still observing. If he is not going to sleep, he might as well do something useful.

He gently lays her head against his folded legs, careful not to wake her, though the girl sleeps like the dead and is doubtless to be roused.

With steady, lithe fingers, he begins to work the knots from her long blonde locks.

# Chapter 17

--------------------------------------------------------------

Cally rises with the dawn, the sun streaking into the small hut in little rays of transparent warmth. The heat of the morning sun is pleasant to her shaded limbs, the fire having burnt out sometime during the night. She arises slowly, awareness returning languidly to her senses.

As she gains consciousness, she notices warmth against her back as well. Actually, perhaps warmth is not quite the correct term. Burning is more accurate; hot, flaming heat along her spine.

Cally jumps awake, her body jolting away from the heat source. She whips around and is startled to see thick, orange flames curling upwards. They lick dangerously at the peak of the tarp tent, precariously close to the tree branches themselves. Cally coughs on the smoke as she looks frantically for an exit.

That's when her eyes alight on the very source of the problem itself. Atlas sits on the other side of the raging fire, his eyes filled with a destructive glee as he watches the flames rise higher and higher. A bundle of dried reeds and twigs are held in his arms, occasionally releasing a few into the fire. Cally has never seen him smile before, but he is very close to it now.

"What are you doing!?" She exclaims, already diving across to take the tinder away from him.

"It gets bigger the more you put in," he says in wonder.

"Yes!" She coughs. "That's how fire works!" She rips the reeds out of his hands, startling him from his pyromaniacal reverie. He looks at her in utter confusion as she grips his wrist and drags him from the smoke-filled tent. He goes with her willingly, wondering what has upset her so.

Once outside, Cally releases his wrist and anxiously turns around. Thankfully, the tent is not on fire, yet, just completely filled with smoke. She bends over, elbows on her knees as she hacks and coughs. Her eyes glance reproachfully up at Atlas, bothered to not see him in a similar state of distress. He looks down at her, arms crossed casually over his chest.

Cally stands up to her full height, still much shorter than he, and jabs a finger in his chest. "Are you insane?!" She asks, eyes fierce with anger. "That's my house! That's my house you nearly burned down! Do you have any idea how dangerous your little stunt was?! You could have killed me." She jabs her finger at him after every clause, bouncing on her toes like a boxer ready to fight. "You--you... pyromaniac you!"

She finishes her rant with an angry scowl. Cally knows she must look at least a little scary. She feels like she could be shooting lasers at him through her eyes. He nearly burned her home to the ground! Her little house would have been nothing but ashes in the sand if she hadn't awoken when she did. For heaven's sake, the man was a menace!

Atlas watches with utmost amusement.

His jaw aches with the effort of keeping the smile from his lips; however, his eyes clearly display the glee in his countenance. Of all the things he has put her through, this is the one she is most upset about. He has never seen her angry like this before and it is his favorite of her emotions thus far. Her tiny hands, fisted at her sides, nearly shake with rage. Her lips pull down into a pout, brows furrowing to form a crease above her nose. She probably is very angry, but to him she is no more threatening than a clam.

Atlas could almost describe her as cute.

"But did it burn down?" He asks, gesturing his arm wide.

Cally's bravado cracks. "Well, no, but--"

"Did I?"

"That's not the point!"

"But what if it was?"

"You are insufferable!" She shouts. "What if you had burned m--" All of the sudden, she stops. As though she had been doused in a bucket of cold water, Cally's entire body tenses as she realizes her mistake. In her rush of adrenaline, she had forgotten who it was she had been speaking to. She had forgotten that she was speaking--was insulting--the very man who held her fate in his hands.

"I-I'm sorry. I shouldn't... Shouldn't have..."

Atlas advances towards her a step, craning his head down to meet her lowering gaze.

"You were going to ask what would happen if you had been burned, correct?" His voice is low, steady.

"I..." Cally wrings her hands together behind her back, tucking her chin away from him. "I for... forgot--"

"Forgot what, to be afraid of me?" He asks, bending down to look into her eyes. He holds eye-contact for a long moment until she breaks it. Cally's shoulders inch up to her ears, shrinking herself even smaller. He places a finger under her chin, lifting her gaze up to meet his own. "I wouldn't have let anything happen to you."

Her eyes widen, lips parting at the unexpected statement. They fill with a little light she had lost over the many weeks spent alone.

"Honestly, I've put way too much effort into keeping you alive. I can't let anything happen to you after all the time I've spent on your safety." His reply is blunt and callous, but somewhat comforting nevertheless. Despite not having the best intentions, the point is still the same: he wouldn't have hurt her.

Cally takes a deep breath as Atlas retracts his had. She swallows, the fear that had taken over her thoughts slowly dissipating. A long silence is drawn out between them, during which Atlas remains astute to her passing emotions. Confusion first overtakes her countenance, followed by resignation, then finally settling on peace.

"Just please be careful with the fire next time? It's dangerous," she says quietly, evenly.

"You should at least thank me before you go patronizing me," Atlas quips.

"Thank you? For doing what?" She asks, crossing her arms defensively.

Atlas chuckles mockingly. "Oh, don't tell me you didn't even notice."

"Notice wha--"

Atlas reaches a hand forward, ignoring Cally's flinch. His fingers delicately stroke her hair from her temple all the way down her long, flowing golden tresses. His fingers glide smoothly and without the tug of a single knot or tangle.

Cally first watches him with apprehension then with shock. "Did you..."

"It looked awful, so I decided to fix it. I think I did a rather sufficient job of it. Plus, you didn't even wake," Atlas admits as he pulls away.

"You... You touched me in my sleep?" She asks with mild anger.

"When else would I have done it?" He parries. "You flinch at my every movement," he snaps his fingers in front of her nose, receiving the desired result. "See?"

Cally is momentarily at a loss for words. She frowns at him, more than a little disturbed by his reasoning. "And that is a reasonable excuse?" She asks. "I have every reason to be wary of your actions, especially actions which include the handling of my body."

Atlas tsks sarcastically. "So ungrateful..."

"You could have at least asked for my permission. It is what most people do."

"Most people as in humans, correct?" He crosses his arms over his chest, an aloof look taking over his countenance. "Oh, so you humans are so much better, huh? Such perfect little do-no-wrong animals."

"It is human culture to ask before touching someone, yes," Cally defends. "There are some who break those rules, but usually we stick to the idea that you only touch someone with permission."

Atlas narrows his eyes. "What do you mean? If it is in your culture to ask for such things, why do some ignore that?"

Cally draws a blank, not exactly sure how to explain. He has a point, but unfortunately things aren't always that simple. "Yes, but there are some humans who think they are above those rules. They think they have the right to override someone's words."

He takes a moment to ponder her words before responding: "Does this happen often?" He momentarily forgets about their current argument.

"Do you remember the conversation we had--what you warned me about--the first night you were... Had two legs?" Cally asks.

"Yes." he replies slowly, understanding where her thoughts are leading.

"Some human men behave the same way--"

"What are you saying?" He asks harshly. "That we are somehow comparable?"

"Yes," Cally bravely replies. "Not all humans do such despicable things, but some do and of varying degree, just like your kind would do to me."

"Our actions are excusable. We would never do those things to our own people. You humans are our prey, which gives us the right--"

"No, it doesn't!" Cally harshly replies. "Whether it is against your own people or another's, the actions are still the same. It is disgusting and wrong for both parties regardless of biological makeup." Cally feels the sting of tears behind her eyes, a result of the heavy emotions waying on her psyche. "Humans are capable of terrible things, just as your kind are capable of terrible things. But my people are also capable of doing good." Her voice grows softer, eyes looking up to his dark, hooded ones. "Just like I'm sure your people can do good as well, I just don't think I've had the opportunity to see it yet."

Atlas remains emotionless to her eyes, but his insides twist with anxiety. Everything that he has ever convinced himself of is being dissolved thought by thought through the words of a creature he never imagined himself capable of conversing with. His mental image of humans crumbles before his eyes as the reality of her words ring true.

"So you see, then," she whispers softly, intimately. She steps closer, throwing him off with her uncharacteristic bravery. "We are not quite as different as we may seem."

Atlas observes her from the opposite side of the fire. She sits silently, occasionally tending to the flames which flicker in the darkness. Her countenance is one of peace and serenity. No harsh lines of anger mar her brow, no signs of sadness or grief twist her lips. Malice is no where to be found, only sublime tranquility.

After everything she has been through--everything he has put her through--she remains resilient. She still grieves for the things taken away from her, he has witnessed her moments of weakness, yet she still has the goodness--the love--to accept his kind as capable of virtuous acts. It is baffling, to say the least. He has done nothing to provoke her acceptance, yet he has gained it nonetheless.

She lays her head to rest, eyelids closing softly, lashes brushing cheeks turned rosy by the sun. Soon her breaths even, her chest rising and falling. Atlas listens to the steady beat of her heart as it thrums repeatedly in her chest. The soothing sound almost lulls him into a slumber of his own, but he forces himself to remain awake.

He has a human to protect, after all.

# Chapter 18

-------------------------------------------------------------

Cally has not seen Atlas in many hours. After retrieving her breakfast he had taken his leave and she has not seen him since. Of course, his whereabouts shouldn't be of any consequence to her, yet she can't help feeling exposed without his presence.

Ever since she awoke this morning she had felt the tightening grip of foreboding weighing on her chest. Even now the feeling grows ever stronger. Part of her wants to ignore the feeling, knowing it is probably a fluke in her senses from spending so much time alone in a frightening landscape. Yet, she has also only felt this way once before. That day just so happened to be the day she was taken by Atlas. Having such a record of sixth-sense foreshadowing, she finds it difficult to push the oppressive feelings away. Although, perhaps that difficulty is for good reason.

This is exactly why she wishes to find Atlas. Despite him being the main reason for her troubles, he has also proven on multiple accounts that he would protect her. Only, protect her from what she is not sure. Cally's brain wracks itself for an answer to that question. If she knew what danger would be happening, then it would be easier to prepare herself. Unfortunately, her senses offer no such clarity.

She also wonders to what extent Atlas' protective nature would go. So far, he has provided her with sustenance, saved her from drowning, and given his word that he would let no harm befall her by his hand. But what about at the hand of another? Would he save her then? With the respect he has for his kind, she doubts he would betray his blood for her sake.

Cally rests her makeshift bucket of water back in the sand after taking a refreshing sip. With little determination--driven mostly by fear for her safety--Cally begins to search for Atlas. There is the high likelihood that he is in the ocean somewhere. This is a place she cannot venture, so she will stick to searching the island first.

It is small, so it will only take her about an hour to hike the entire perimeter. That would leave only the inland circle left to search afterwards.  Cally begins her trek, thankful for the hat and longsleave shirt she discovered in the suitcase. Her fair skin has suffered greatly in the past weeks and she is more thankful than ever for the fully covering items.

Soon enough, sweat begins to gather on the back of her neck and along the rim of her hat despite the ocean breeze. Taking a break from her hike, she treads a few paces into the surf to cool herself before trudging back up to the drier sand. She remains close to the water, though; the powdery sand being much too hot to walk on in bare feet. Cally also unbuttons the top few buttons of her white shirt, the breeze blowing into and around her torso nicely.

As she searches, occasionally calling his name, she begins to wonder if maybe seeking his protection was selfish. Would being near him put him in danger as well? No, he owes her this much at least. Yet, Cally can't help feeling bad about the possibility of him getting hurt on her account. Then again, all of this is his fault anyways. If only Cally weren't so forgiving, maybe she could not feel so responsible for him, but alas, her heart is too kind.

Large rocks and boulders rise occasionally from the sand, the sight beautiful despite being her prison. For what seems like the hundredth time, Cally wishes she had a camera to capture the scene. No doubt her mother would love to see it, and Ethan would have the grandest time climbing and playing on the natural jungle-gym.

Those happy thoughts soon turn into a dull ache in her chest. She tends to avoid thinking of them, yet sometimes she still finds herself unable to block her loved ones from her thoughts. She wonders how they must be doing. It has been weeks since her disappearance, have they lost hope in finding her yet? She wants them to have not given up, that they are still ardently searching for her, but at the same time she wishes they would move on. As much as she wants to be rescued, she also does not want them to suffer her loss any longer than they need to.

Lost so deeply in her thoughts, Cally should have been paying more attention to her surroundings.

Perhaps then she would have realized she was no longer alone on the island.

Footsteps disguised by the sound of breaking waves, the creature followed after her. Cally never noticed their arrival, and had no inclination of the follower she had picked up until they were only a few paces behind her.

A cloud passes overhead, casting the island in shadow. Hairs pricked on the back of Cally's neck, goosebumps rising along her arms despite the heat. Her sweat turned cold as her footsteps came to a grinding halt, heartbeat now audible to her own ears and that of another.

Cally remains frozen in her place, too afraid to run and lacking the courage to turn around. Lips apart, eyes wide with trembling knees as all other sounds die away. She breathes softly, listening closely. In. Out. In. Out. One footstep. Two footsteps. Three. The wind goes silent.

"Did no one ever tell you how dangerous these water were?" A voice, low and seductive... Unfamiliar. "Or were you brave enough to venture here alone?" He tsks. Cally feels him come closer, held captive by her fear. "What a grave mistake you have made, little human," he whispers to her softly.

Cally rotates on legs filled with led. Her gaze inches up, up, up to the face of the man--creature before her. She recognizes what he is instantly. Skin ghostly white, teeth too sharp to be human, and stark naked. His smile is wicked--vicious--she can already see her blood dripping from his lips in her mind's eyes. No doubt he can too.

Cally runs the hardest she ever has before, legs moving faster than she thought herself capable of doing. The sand grasps at her feet, betraying her as it prohibits her flight. She hears him laughing behind her, the sound echoing in her ears. The terrain grows more difficult as rocks, fallen palms, and driftwood mar the sandy beach. She finds herself jumpimg over rocks and boulders, their sun-baked surface stinging her skin.

Her arms and legs ache with the effort of climbing and running. Her fear produces as much adrenaline as possible, but she can feel her body slowing anyways. Heart thudding in her chest, carbon dioxide escapes her lungs in ragged gasps. No doubt her hands and feet are bleeding by now, but she ignores it.

Climbing over another large stone, her body goes crashing to its surface as a hand clamps around her ankle, yanking her backwards and dragging her down the slope. Cally cries out as the jagged stone rakes across her skin and catches on her clothes. She feels her body being pulled backwards and thrown into the unforgiving sand.

Before she can even think about standing back up, a heavy weight settles over her body. Cally kicks her legs and thrashes as hands grasp her flailing arms, pinning them down. She screams as fear and claustrophobia settle in her bones. She feels it before she hears it, blinding pain exploding over the right side of her face. An echoing slap sounds afterwards as stars dance across her vision.

She goes limp as her body fails to gather enough energy to fight back. She blinks her eyes to see the creature looming over her. He smirks maliciously as a look of eminent death fills his gaze. His eyes rake over her body and Cally wishes she hadn't unbuttoned her shirt.

"Give up so easily?" He asks. His face grows closer to her exposed neck. "But I was having so much fun chasing you!"

Cally whimpers as his tongue runs lazily up the side of her neck. "Atlas! Atlas please!" Is the only thing she can think to scream. "Help me!" Her voice screeches hoarsely.

Hands wander her body to places she had never been touched before. Tears sting her eyes as she wiggles and kicks uselessly beneath the creature above her. She screams in agony as teeth latch around her collar bone and bite harshly into her skin.

Cally calls for the only safety she knows, yet she loses hope by the second. She kicks at him again only to earn another blow to her face, knocking her head back into the sand.

Atlas' feet pound into the sand as he races down the beach.

He easily clears rocks and debris as his legs carry him forwards ever faster. His kind's biological advantage has never been more useful as he pushes his body to its limits.

He returned from the sea only to find shed scales and blood only a day old, and it wasn't his. They were no longer alone on the island. When he reached the hut to warn Cally, she was no where to be found, dread instantly settling in his chest.

Atlas wasted no time in running after her, and that's when he heard her screams. He has been running after her for too long now, her screams having gone silent. Faster, he urges himself. Faster or she will be dead.

He leaps over a final fallen tree before he sees her pinned to the sand. His entire body shakes as a livid rage takes over him. A male holds her to the ground as he licks the blood from her exposed chest, her white linen shirt discarded to the side. Her face is red and wet with tears, eyes screwed shut as barely audible whimpers slip past bloody lips.

Just when Cally thought it would get worse than she could recover from, his weight is suddenly lifted from her body completely. Her eyes fly open to see the creature ripped away from her by a man--a man in brown khaki shorts with familiar black hair. Cally scrambles for her shirt as she crawls away from a scene she would never forget.

The creature is quick to hop back on his feet as Atlas advances towards him. The two males circle each other, gazes the complete opposite of each other. The creature smirks mockingly as Atlas wears a look of predatory rage like no other. He continues to pace, fists clenching at his sides as he eyes his opponent.

"I didn't know the human was claimed," the other male chuckles, blue eyes watching Atlas for a reaction. Atlas does not respond. The creature casts his gaze to the girl cowering only a few meters away.

"Don't look at her," Atlas' voice is deep, commanding, and completely unlike anything Cally has ever heard from him. It thoroughly chills her to the bone as she continues to watch the two males with renewing fear.

"Or what?" The other replies. "I'm willing to share, if that's what you want," he bargains.

Atlas snarles like a dog gone feral. "She is mine!"

The creature's gaze turns cold. "Then so be it."

The two fly at each other like the apex predators they are. Claws reaching for a throat are dodged at the last second, catching a shoulder instead. Atlas throws his shoulder into the other male as they go crashing to the ground. He loses control as the other ends up on top of him, throwing one, two, three punches before Atlas catches his hand and slashes his chest.

Blood sprays across his face as the creature screeches in pain. They roll a few times, each landing various strikes to the other as they both fight for dominance. Atlas is able to slash at the male's neck, sending the creature recoiling. He uses the opportunity to pull himself out from beneath him and wrap his legs around the male's neck. He reaches for an arm and pulls it up tight against his chest as he holds the creature down. The other male uses his free hand to reach around and claws at Atlas' back, raking all the way from neck to hip. He cries out in pain as he loses his grip on his opponent's hand.

Atlas lays still in the sand as blood drips from his wounds. The male untangles himself and Atlas' stomach explodes in white-hot pain as a foot drives itself below his ribs. He sees the other male walking threateningly towards Cally. Atlas grits his teeth.

He forces himself to stand, the wounds on his back stinging as they stretch. Without wasting another moment on his own pain he launches himself at the other male. They go tumbling to the sand once more and Atlas wraps his body around the creature as tightly as possible. The male claws and kicks but Atlas holds fast, reaching his arms around his neck.

With a sharp jerk of his arms and a twist, the creature's neck snaps.

His body goes limp and Atlas releases him slowly. He stands on weak legs, right arm wrapping around his bruised stomach. He sneers at the dead body below him before stepping over it.

He stumbles to Cally where she cowers in the shade of a boulder. His voice is hoarse and deep when he speaks.

"Calliope?"

# Chapter 19

"Calliope?"

Cally is too overwhelmed to fully process that this is the first time he has spoken her full name. Fear, apprehension, relief, and exhaustion are all present in her current state. She watches Atlas warily as he sways on his feet. Blood covers him completely, making him more horrific looking than she has ever seen but also more heroic.

She can't imagine what her fate would have been had he not saved her, and not only did he stop him, but put an end to him completely. Cally shivers as she eyes the dead body only a few yards away. Part of her feels sorry for his death, but the majority is glad of it. She wouldn't wish death on anyone, but he would have killed her had Atlas not done what he did.

"Don't look," Atlas commands, seeing her face pale the longer she gazes at the corpse. He steps towards her yet she backs away instantly. He frowns, confusion lacing his tone. "What's wrong?"

"I..." she clutches her torn shirt around herself tighter, hands trembling as her lip wobbles. "What you said..."

"...Is what I had to," he finishes. "You are mine in that you are my responsibility. Nothing more."

Cally slumps down against the rock behind her, a weight she wasn't aware of lifting from her chest. She nods slowly as tears trail down her cheeks. With that thought now out of her mind, everything else she feels has room to come forward.

Atlas watches her crumble into a ball of tears in the sand. She is still wearing the cotton pants but her shirt is torn and wrapped around her haphazardly. Blood is smeared all down her front, cuts and scrapes still bleeding. He kneels before her, eyes and countenance made as soft as he can manage.

"He hurt you," he observes. He gulps, not wanting to push her to recount what happened any more than she needs to, but also needing to be sure. "Where?"

She raises her gaze to his slowly, his image made blurry by her tears. She shakes her head, ducking her chin back down to her chest. She does not wish to answer, so she hopes he will drop the question. He does not, however, and she curles herself tighter at the sound of his voice.

"Cally, you need to tell me. Did I get here in time?" He asks. She looks up at him in confusion, not understanding his exact meaning. "You know what I mean," he answers.

Oh.

"N-no I..." a sniffle. "I'm okay."

Atlas releases a breath he hadn't realized he was holding. His body aches in protest as he reaches a hand towards her. She only stares at his open hand for many moments, before slowly sliding her hand into his. His grip is warm and gentle, fingers wrapping delicately around her own.

He pulls her up to standing, where she immediately tightens her shirt once more. Atlas looks away though her body is still completely covered. He understands her concern. Her knees shake as she stands, clutching his arm as tightly as possible for balance. He suppresses a hiss as her grip squeezes one of his many bruises.

"Can you walk?" He asks.

She frowns, then looks up at him. "Can you?"

"I'll be fine," he grumbles.

"Then so will I."

Together they slowly make their way up the beach. They help each other over and around debris as neither of them are exactly strong enough to do so on their own. Throughout the journey, Cally never loses her hold on Atlas, hands always holding onto him in some way or another. Her grip is sometimes painful but Atlas never says a word.

The trip is long and by the time they reach home, the sun is just setting below the horizon. Stars blink to light as the strip of sky along the ocean steadily turns from orange, to pink, to finally purple. It is so beautiful it almost seems like it could erase the horrors witnessed only a few hours prior.

Atlas and Cally finally enter the tent after a very long and painful hike. They both breathe sighs of relief as they rest on their opposite sides of the campfire. They rest only a moment before they part their separate ways to tend to they own duties. Cally changes her clothes while Atlas gathers wood for the fire.

After a fire is made, Atlas glances around for Cally. Only, he does not find her. He pokes his head outside the tent to see her stumbling through the sand with multiple items in her hands. He holds the flap open as she ducks inside, letting her many objects fall to the ground.

Atlas observes her in utter confusion as she sits cross-legged beside him. "What are you doing?" He asks.

"Well, we can't just stay like this," she answers. "We need to get cleaned up somehow."

She places a bar of soap on a smooth rock and a torn piece of T-shirt beside it. She also sets down a small bucket of water. She then grabs the soap, but before she can place it in the water, a hand grasps her wrist.

"What are you doing?" He asks. "That's your drinking water."

Cally rolls her eyes. "I know that, but I need to use it anyways. Besides, it looks like it might rain tomorrow." Atlas releases her reluctantly. She clears her throat almost awkwardly. "Could you, um, turn around?" She asks timidly.

Atlas looks at the small amount of water in the pail before looking back at her. "Don't waste your water," he says. "Wash yourself."

"No."

Atlas frowns. "What?"

"I said no. So, turn around."

Atlas is too tired to argue further.

He rotates slowly, unsurely. One of the first things he ever learned was to never turn your back to someone, he has even told Cally that before, and now he is doing just that. He waits impatiently for her to begin.

Atlas is startled by the cool water as the fabric is run over his marred skin. When he had been expecting pain, he found no such thing. Instead, her strokes were delicate and gentle, working their best to go between the many lacerations on his back and shoulders.

"This is going to hurt," he hears her say. He hisses as she gently pours some of the water over his back, washing the suds from his skin and the sand from his cuts. Soon she is finished, and he turns back to face her.

Having her in his sight once again, his eyes are immediately drawn to the blood on her own skin. He goes to take the cloth from her, but she snatches it back.

"I can clean myself," she answers his questioning gaze quietly.

"I know," he replies. "But I can help."

"I-I um, I don't want to be touched," she mumbles. "Especially not where he did."

Atlas chooses not to respond, turning to the fire and giving her his back for privacy. He had wanted to help her like she had helped him, and he was rejected. He understood her reasoning, but he couldn't help feeling dejected that she didn't trust him even after everything he had done to save her.

She finishes soon enough, returning the items then making her way to her side of the fire. She curles up on her side with her knees pulled tightly to her chest. Her body still shudders and her mind is still foggy from shock, but slowly she is regaining her recollection of the events that had transpired.

She presses her palm over her mouth  to repress a sob from escaping. His invading breath on her neck, his roaming hands, the punches, all of it she remembers like a horror movie playing on repeat behind her closed eyelids. The fear and hopelessness she felt were just as suffocating as his body weighing her down. Even now she wishes she were standing just so she didn't feel so exposed.

Mind refusing to shut down, her eyes stayed open, actively searching the darkness for any danger. She was unable to stop herself from keeping a watchful eye on her surroundings. Never again would she be caught unawares.

She hugs her legs up close to her chest and rocks herself silently. Now more than ever she wishes for the comforting presence of a closed, and locked, door. She wishes she had her parents to be in the room down the hall to protect her. She wishes...

Cally slowly turns to see Atlas on the other side of the fire, eyes staring intently into the flames. He is completely still and silent, gaze occasionally surveying the area before resting back on the fire.

Cally remembers she is not alone. She is not alone and there is someone to protect her. They may not fully trust each other yet, but he is there to save her nonetheless. She stares at him quietly, a thought brewing in her mind the longer she stares.

Cally rises slowly from her spot and makes her way around the fire. Without saying a word, she lays herself down beside him, head towards his side and back to the warmth of the fire. She settles in comfortably, feeling more protected than she has in a long time.

It doesn't take long for her to fall asleep. Atlas waits as her breaths begin to steady and her eyelids flutter shut. Her lips part softly and her shoulders relax as she finally succumbs to a deep slumber. The only part of her body that does not relax is her hand which cleanches tightly by her chest.

Carefully, gently, he slides his fingers around her's, loosening them from their tight grasp. She curles her fingers around his of her own accord, and he lets her. Atlas holds her hand as she sleeps quietly, both feeling more at peace than they have in a very long time.

# Chapter 20



Atlas puts all of his strength into heaving the log further up the beach. His joints and muscles ache in protest, his wounds from the day before stretching and reopening. He welcomes the pain, as it is the perfect distraction from his whirling, hate-filled thoughts.

He releases his anger by hammering stakes through the wooden logs, though it does little to diminish his fury. He is blinded by so much hatred and guilt he can hardly see straight, the task at hand being the only thing to keep him from going insane with rage.

Self hatred burns in his chest like the hottest flames, burning him from the inside out with guilt and shame. His breaths are laboured both from the physical activity and the strength it takes to ignore the pain from his wounds. His back feels as though it is being ripped apart all over again each time he reaches for another log. The pain is good, though; maybe he deserves it.

He had grown sick watching the human girl for so long. The longer he stared at her the worse her injuries seemed to look. He can only imagine how horrible they would be--how much she would have lost--had he not saved her. Yet, at the same time, how bad would her wounds be if he hadn't kidnapped her at all?

She wouldn't have any.

He picks up another log.

He had stared at her so long he got to where he couldn't look another second. He ignored her hand reaching for his as he rose and left the tent. He knew exactly how he could fix his mistake, so that's exactly what he did.

It was still dark when he left the tent, the moon still high in the sky. He was wary of leaving her unaccompanied, so he never strayed far. Every now and then he would return to check on the girl, making sure she was still sleeping soundly. Each time she was exactly as he had left her, fast asleep and curled by the fire.

All of this, everything that had befallen her was his fault. He knew at the beginning that his actions were wrong, but he was too afraid to admit it to himself. Coward. He had only wanted to make someone pay. He wanted to do unto them as they had done unto him. It was payback, a penalty to the human race for everything they had taken from him.

Only, he hadn't realized he had lowered himself to their level of inferiority in doing so. In aiming for justice he had made himself no better than they had been. He had been so controlled by hate it blinded him from the consequences of his actions.

Now every time his looks at Calliope all he sees is what had been done to her. Atlas became no better than the very men who destroyed his childhood and taken her away from him. Humans had taken the most important thing in his life, someone innocent and kind. Now Atlas had done the same.

He continues to work on his project, placing the various logs and branches in their allotted places before fastening them together with reeds and vines. It will be some time before it can be put to use, but it will indeed be useful. Maybe then he will have redeemed himself in some small way.

"Atlas? Atlas!" He hears her voice call. Even from here he can sense the anxiousness in her tone.

Without another moment's thought he dashes back to the hut. He arrives just as she stumbles out, eyes searching and hands trembling. Concern fills his countenance as he reaches her, wondering what could have possibly happened in such a short period time since he last checked her.

"Did something happen?" He asks instantly, standing only an arm's length away from her.

The sight of him slowly calms her down to a more rational state. Her arms secure around herself as she fumbles for an answer. "I... no, nothing happened. I just, um, didn't see you when I woke up."

Atlas instantly realizes his mistake. "I didn't leave you, I swear. I was only working just over there," he says, gesturing to his project laying a little farther down the beach.

A light bit of pink reaches Cally's cheeks as embarrassment heats her neck and ears. All of her irrational worries were for nothing. He had no reason to stay all night with her anyways. "Its alright. I was just being stupid," she mumbles.

Atlas does not reply, as he isn't exactly sure how to do so. After looking her over once more, he turns and makes his way back to the work still left to finish. Walking further down the beach, he hears the distinct sound of her soft footsteps following after him. He does not mind, as the closer she is the easier it is to keep an eye on her.

"What are you building?" She asks tentatively as he resumes his work. He seats himself at one of the corners, beginning to wrap vines around the junction of logs once more.

"A raft," is his short reply.

A small bubble of hope fills Cally's chest, but she forces herself to not make any assumptions on the matter. "Why..." she swallows thickly. "Why are you building a raft?"

"So I can take you home."

Atlas wasn't sure what he was expecting Cally's reaction to be, but what happened surely was not it. Before he could say anything else, she had completely thrown herself at him. The girl's arms wrapped tightly around his neck as she buried her face in his shoulder. He was at a loss on what to do exactly. One of his arms was pinned againdt him by her torso pressed tightly against his, and the other hung awkwardly at his side.

Cally felt him stiffen instantly, but she refused to let go, instead holding him tighter and letting long awaited tears fall freely. "Th-t hank..." a sob. "Thank you!" The cried more, her shoulders shaking uncontrollably. "S-so much!"

Atlas could feel the tears and snot on his bare skin, but he figured he should let her be. He stayed still as a statue as she cried for many minutes. Eventually, she released him, wiping her nose and then wiping his shoulder with her shirt sleeve as a sheepish expression filled her countenance.

"We will have to wait until the Tide ends before we can depart. I can't make the journey in my human form," he explains.

A smile forms on her lips as she nods her understanding. Ever so slowly, nervousness creeps into her form. Atlas doesn't fail to notice. "Whatever it is you want to ask, just say it," he sighs.

Cally bites her lips anxiously, but obliges nonetheless. "I hope you don't mind my asking, but why did you..." a pause. "Why did you take me?"

Atlas releases a heavy breath, dropping the tools beside him. He knew this question was coming, but he didn't dread it any less. He owes her an answer. Hell, he owes her a lot more than that, but transparency is not one of his virtues.

He sits quietly on the sand, facing the ocean with an unreadable expression. Cally seats herself beside him, offering him both physical and mental space to articulate his answer. It is a while before he speaks.

"My kind never stay long with their young. None of us ever meet our fathers and our mothers only care for us until we are old enough to protect ourselves, usually around eight years." Atlas pauses as he notices her shocked expression, but he doesn't stop to acknowledge it, continuing on. "My mother... She was different. She stayed with me--cared for me--much longer than she needed to.

"Her name was Naya." Atlas chews the inside of his cheek. He had never spoken of her aloud, and the effort proved more difficult to do so than he had imagined it would. "I was nearly thirteen when..." he sighs, running a hand through his dark hair. He doesn't look at Cally--he can't bear to--but he feels her stare, though it isn't one of judgment.

"She had taken us to the surface. It was something we didn't usually do, as it was dangerous being so exposed, but she loved watching the humans. She loved their culture and how they loved each other so much. She taught me about how humans had families. The idea was foreign to me, but I found it just as fascinating as she did.

"We didn't see it coming. There was a boat, a small one, that had nets in the water. When we saw it, we immediately dove for the bottom, but she wasn't fast enough. She was caught in the net and I..." he swallows thickly. "I couldn't get her out in time. She told me to hide, and so I did. I turned and fled.

"When night fell I gained the courage to return to the surface, only to see that the Tide had come. She was in her human form and those males," his fists tremble at his sides. "...They did horrible things to her. I could do nothing but watch as I was too young to have shifted as well. I was trapped in the water unable to save her, only hearing her screaming for them to stop. They eventually killed her, said she was a liability and threw her back in the sea.

"I never forgot their faces. They were even stupid enough to fish the same waters a few years later, so I gave them what they deserved. I had been so angry at all of the human race that when I saw you..." he looks away, forcing himself to release his clenched fists. "I thought you would be the perfect payback. I took you from your family just like my mother was taken from me. I wanted to kill you. I would have, but I couldn't. So, I kept you. I figured that if I didn't give you death then you deserved imprisonment.

"I was mistaken. I failed to realize I had become more than the victim, but also the murderer. I... I almost let you receive the same fate my mother had." He looked at her then, more sincere than he ever had been before. "I won't let you suffer any longer Calliope. I will take you home. I swear no more harm will ever befall you under my care."

Slow, steady tears fell silently down Cally's rosy cheeks. The pain he had gone through was something she could not imagine, even more so on her own. She understood now why he behaves the way he does. She understands her purpose is on the island. Though she does not agree that it is good that she is here, she understands why.

Once more, she pulls him into a hug, though this time with less enthusiasm. She holds him gently, carefully, laying her head on his shoulder. "Humans give each other hugs when we are sad," she explains.

Ever so slowly, Atlas places his hands on her back. He does so gingerly and with much hesitancy, but Cally is grateful for his acceptance nonetheless.

"I am not sad," he says.

"But I am," Cally sniffles.

With a final squeeze, she pulls away from him. Atlas slides a little farther away from her, not exactly as comfortable in her presence as he once was. Cally notices, but makes no objection.

The two stare at the crashing waves, the morning sun rising higher and higher in the sky. The breeze is cool and welcoming on their skin as they sit in silence. Both are lost on their separate thoughts, but they are also at peace. Cally finally has an answer for a question she has had for quite some time. Atlas has found peace with himself at last, a burden lifted.

"Thank you for telling me," she says at last. "I will not condone your actions as far as why I am here, but I thank you for being willing to correct those wrongs."

"I will not ask your forgiveness," he replies. "I only ask that you allow my presence to ensure your safety."

Cally smiles gently at him, small and understanding. "I accept."

# Chapter 21

Atlas lays flat on his stomach, a pain worse than anything he has ever experienced coating the entirety of his upper body. The sand sticking to his chest and arms prevent him from moving in any direction, the tiny grains digging into his inflamed skin with every twitch of his muscles. Atlas knows this is a less than defensive position, but he can't bring himself to sit up.

Cally is currently bathing, so he couldn't follow her there anyways. This allowed him the time to relax on his own, or more accurately, wallow in his pain. This is unlike anything he has experienced before and awaits impatiently for Cally's return. He tells himself he wishes for her presence so he can once more keep an eye on her, but the truth is that he hopes she has an answer to whatever ails him.

Soon enough, he hears soft footfalls padding lightly on the sand. He releases a long held breath as Cally's slight form slips in through the flap of the tent. Her eyes immediately flick to his form, and he is startled to see them widen in horror upon seeing his body.

"I told you to come inside earlier yesterday," she accuses, kneeling by his side.

"What are you talking about?"

"Yesterday when you were working on the raft I said you should take a break and finish it tomorrow. You replied something along the lines of I know what I'm doing, but clearly I was right."

Atlas groans, letting his head fall against the sandy floor. "I don't see how that has anything to do with this... with this problem."

"You have a sunburn," Cally deadpans. "Your skin is so translucently white I'm surprised this hasn't happened before."

Atlas grunts in reply.

"Just... stay here a moment. I'll get you something."

He grunts again.

Exiting the tent, Cally shakes her head with a small chuckle. He gets points for being determined, but his stubbornness got in the way. She retrieves a small bottle of lotion kept in the chest, still forever thankful for its discovery.

When she returns, Atlas is still in a prone position. Her expression morfs into pity the longer she gazes at his red and swollen skin. He will be lucky if it doesn't blister. She kneels gingerly by his side, hesitant to begin applying the lotion.

"Is it alright if I spread this on your back?" She asks.

"Will it make it feel any better?" He replies.

"Well, yes, it will feel better afterwards, but it might hurt when I touch you."

Atlas releases a long, drawn out breath. Perhaps a little temporary pain will be worth the eventual relief. He clenches his fists into the sand, his eyes squeezing shut. "Alright," he mutters.

Cally squeezes a single line down the center of his back. Atlas almost flinches at the cool feeling. Cally takes a deep breath before gingerly laying her hands on his upper back, tentatively rubbing circles into the inflamed skin.

Atlas refuses to let himself squirm as the pressure of her hands stings worse than the tentacles of a jellyfish. The substance is cold and soothing beyond relief, but the weight of her palms is less than welcome. Cally notices his fists clenching in the sand and she cringes internally. She has mixed feelings about her current situation.

She has never done anything like this for anyone else. The closest she has ever been to something like this is applying sunscrean to her younger brother's back. This is entirely different. Part of her feels wrong in a way for venturing to do something like this. She would never touch her male friends like this. Cally was always a girl to keep her hands to herself. She hadn't even had a boyfriend for goodness sakes! And here she is, spreading lotion on the back of an adult male. But does she even consider Atlas a friend? No, they are far from friends. The two are reluctant companions at best. He did kidnap her, after all.

Perhaps that is why she finds this easier to do than with someone she had befriended. Maybe this is one of those instances where it is better with a stranger than someone you know, just like giving a speech to strangers is easier than speaking in front of family.

Yes, that is most likely.

"Why hasn't this happened to you?" Atlas suddenly speaks up, his voice laced with resentment.

"Oh, it has, just not as bad. And besides, I was already tan, re-member? That protects me from burns, unlike your pale skin."

"Its not pale anymore," he grumbles.

Cally chuckles, shaking her head at his words. "No, it isn't."

"Its not funny," Atlas whines. "I don't see how any of this could be perceived as humorous."

Cally laughs openly then, her head thrown back just the slightest. "Oh, yes, it's quite funny. You are probably redder than my dad was two summers ago..."

Cally's hands suddenly still as her voice trails off. Atlas rotates his head up to glance back at her to see the girl's eyes turned away from him, staring at the flames with a far away look in her stormy grey eyes. He then realizes her change of mood.

"You will see them again. I promised you that," he voices, breaking her from her nostalgic trance.

Cally shakes her head, as if to rid her mind of unwanted thoughts. "I know, I just... couldn't help it."

Her hands begin their work once more, smoothing over the crest of his shoulders and down the backs of his arms. Atlas knows he should say something, but comforting others is not one of his few virtues. He has upset her. Not directly, as it was her words not his own that troubled her, but the thoughts were instigated by him.

"Tell me about them," he says. Perhaps this was not the best thing to ask, but he is also curious. He never had a family.

The cool morning air blows in through the tent flap, breezing over the fire and toying with a strand of Cally's hair. She brushes it aside as she ponders what to say. She has avoided speaking about them to save her feelings, but perhaps it is time she remember them, especially now that she knows she will see them once more.

"My dad isn't the most outdoorsy. He works as an engineer and is often holed up in his office at home. My mom is your typical housewife, doing the cooking, cleaning, grocery shopping and such. They will have been married twenty years this winter."

Atlas hasn't heard of most of the things she speaks of, but he remains silent. He will ask later.

"I only have one sibling, my brother. He is younger than me by ten years as my parents weren't really expecting another child. They had originally planned to only have me, but obviously that didn't happen. I remember when they told me I was going to be an older sister," a broad smile fills her face. "I was positively ecstatic.

"We have practically been inseparable ever since he was old enough to toddle after me. In a way, I was also one of his parents. Mom and dad doted on him a lot and gave him what he wanted, but if he ever really needed anything he would always come to me first. I'm not sure why. Maybe we just share a more comfortable bond with each other than we do with our parents."

She has long since forgotten her task and has probably gone over the same spot on his back at least four times now, yet Atlas stays silent. He has never heard someone speak with as much love as Cally does when she describes her family. He can't help feeling the slightest pang of jealousy. She has something he could never even dream of obtaining.

"You say your parents are married. Is that a human custom?" He asks his first question.

"Oh, yes. When we find someone we love, we have a ceremony called a wedding. The two people who love each other make vows and promises to love each other forever and to be true to each other. It is a holy pact to remain faithful and devoted to your partner," her smile turns longing. "It is a truly beautiful thing."

Atlas ponders her words. "Do all humans do this? You never take more than one lover in a lifetime?"

Cally bites her lip. "Well, no. Most do get married, yes, but some-times their spouse dies, or they fall out of love and separate. Others don't get married at all."

Atlas frowns. "This saddens you."

Cally shakes her head. "No... well, I guess it does make me sad." She removes her hands and rests her elbows on her knees, getting list in voicing her thoughts. "It is just something I've never really understood."

"How do you mean?" Atlas asks, ever the curious one.

"Marriage is meant to be holy and beautiful, the two full of love and respect for their spouse, yet there are those who lose the beauty of marriage somewhere along the way. Sometimes people realize they never loved each other in the first place or they find the person they married wasn't who they thought they were. Others treat weddings as social gatherings or displays of wealth instead of intimate ceremonies, the vows as breakable promises and not words of bonding. I guess I just feel like too many people take love for granted."

Her words are spoken with such passion and soul that Atlas can't help agreeing with her. He does not entirely understand or agree with the concept, but her words ring with a truth that is hard to ignore.

Atlas rises to a sitting position, dusting the sand from his chest. "My people do not marry. Most of us don't even have lovers, only those we mate with to ensure the continuation of our species."

"That is unfortunate," Cally voices with all sincerity.

"Yes," his voice is low and quiet, almost blown away by the breeze. "I believe you are right." A pause. "Do you wish to marry?"

Cally smiles, then a nod. "I can't imagine anything more pleasing. To have someone completely and totally dedicated to you just as much as you are them... is there anything more securing than that?"

Atlas doesn't have an answer. He asks a different question: "What if you don't find someone who will love you?"

"I don't know," she answers. "There are many people in this world. I'm sure I will find someone eventually."

Atlas nods, tossing a small twig into the fire. "You said your parents hadn't planned to have another child. Is it normal for married people to choose the number of children they wish to have?"

"Yes, actually," she replies. "Most couples long discuss that before they even get married."

"How many children do you want?" He asks.

"I want three," she says without hesitation. "Two boys and then a girl, but I can't exactly pick their genders. I will be happy with however many children I am given, but in a perfect world that would be my choice."

Atlas observes her tranquil smile and relaxed state. This is something she has been planning for a long time and has held in high respect, that much he knows for sure. He had never given children much thought. He would never raise children anyways, but seeing the peace and hope on her face, he can't help entertaining the idea. What would it be like to raise a child? Would it be hard?

He decides to voice his thoughts. "Males of my species never raise children. Is the task difficult?"

Cally purses her lips. "It depends on the age, really, and I'm sure it is quite different for our separate species, and yes, it is difficult, but it seems like the love you receive from a child would be more than worth the effort."

Atlas remembers the love and admiration he had for his mother. Would his child love and adore him like he had his mother?

Cally had never expected to discuss these things with Atlas. She had never really voiced these thoughts to anyone before, and yet she found the conversation comforting. It had felt good to share her thoughts and ideas, especially to someone who would listen with utmost attention and even ask her questions.

She glances over his reddened chest, eyebrows pulling together. He would hurt for days, no doubt, and she wonders if he will get cranky throughout the healing process like she would. Hopefully, he doesn't.

"Here," she says, handing him the bottle. "You will want to put this on your chest."

Atlas glares at the bottle before snatching it up. Cally leaves the tent momentarily, probably to collect firewood for later, and Atlas follows her with his eyes. When she is no longer in sight, he begins setting about tending to his sunburnt chest.

All the while, he wishes it were her delicate hands doing the healing and not his own.

# Chapter 22

With Atlas' sunburn beginning to heal, he has taken to working on the raft once more. Cally usually splits her time between taking walks on the beach--within Atlas' sight, of course--or trying to help him with the raft.

The thing is large and heavy to maneuver, which makes piecing it together quite difficult. When he lifts the logs, she wraps the vines around and underneath it before he places the wood back down again. It is a long and sweaty job so she is thankful when the sun begins to set and the workday is over.

Atlas has taken to the sea to acquire dinner while she was left to stay at camp. She had said she would stay in the tent and watch the fire, but the sweat on her body begs to be removed. Surely she could bathe before he returned, couldn't she?

Cally gathers the necessary soaps before making her way to one of the shallow pools nearby. She places her items on a rock beside her before removing her shirt and shorts. She quickly replaces them with her bikini as she is still too insecure to bathe completely naked despite being alone.

She moves quickly to scrub the soap over her dirty skin, washing away the dreaded sweat and sand. She then retrieves the razor which she had found in the suitcase and begins to slide it over her now deeply tanned legs.

In what is probably not the most logical course of action, Cally begins to rush herself as sunlight steadily fades from the sky. In a rather unlucky way, the razor, which had become dull and near to rusting in the salty air, nicked her knee in a jagged cut. Blood dribbled up from the small injury and slowly trickled down the length of her leg.

She hissed at the sudden pain and went to cover the cut. A little too late, she realized her hands were covered in saltwater which only made it sting more. She blows anxiously at the small cut, ignorant of the trickle of blood that comes dangerously close to dripping into the water.

"WHAT ARE YOU DOING?!" She suddenly hears Atlas cry.

She spins around to see him running down the beach and crashing through the shallow water to reach her. Cally, perplexed by whatever fright has gotten into him, prepares to stand as he reaches her side.

"Don't move!" He shouts.

Cally freezes in her place, fingers grasping tightly to the rock beneath her. "What's wrong?" She asks hesitantly.

Atlas doesn't answer. Instead, he grasps her leg tightly with one hand and catches the dribble of blood with the other. Before Cally can protest, Atlas has lifted her into his arms and carries her back to the beach.

Cally wiggles in his grip, quite uncomfortable against his bare chest, but as begins to move faster she finds herself clutching her arms tightly around his neck. "Atlas, what is going on?" She wonders aloud and quite annoyedly.

Atlas stops suddenly once he reaches dry sand. His gaze pins itself on the human girl who clings to him uncomfortably tight. He doesn't answer her question, but instead laughs a low, mocking laugh of disbelief.

Much to Cally's confusion, Atlas carries her all the way back to the tent. He doesn't slow his pace until he stops to place her down gently by the fire.

"My kind can scent out a single drop of blood within only three miles." Atlas grasps her injured leg firmly and guides it into the light of the fire.

Cally swallows thickly, eyes drifting to the blood smeared on her skin by Atlas' hands. His gaze is piercing as the man watches her with disappointment.

He shakes his head, voice hard and reproachful as he speaks. "Even now I can smell the blood flowing through those youthful veins of yours--hear your heart pumping in your chest. This..." he strokes his thumb beside the oozing crimson  wound on her knee. "...Would attract dozens..."

"I'm sorry," Cally cuts in, more afraid of Atlas' words than she had been in a long time.

"Do you really forget?" He continues, voice louder and more urgent, not even acknowledging her words. He takes her wrist in his much larger hand, turning it over to reveal fading purple bruises in the shape of fingers printed into the soft skin of her inner arm.

His voice turns softer, eyes intending to meet hers, but instead getting stuck on her neck where pinprick cuts are now revealed in her state of undress. "Do you really forget what could happen?"

Cally sniffles, swiping her nose with her free hand. "I hadn't meant it," she says. "It was only a simple accident."

"Simple accidents can get you killed," Atlas answers severely. He sighs, reaching up for Cally's cheek. He swipes his fingers delicately under her eyes, catching the tears she hadn't noticed were there. Atlas has done this before, but the circumstances now are far different than they were then. He hadn't meant to make her cry this time.

"Stop that," he whispers quietly.

"I'm sorry," she says again, this time for her tears.

Atlas sighs. "You're not stopping. What is it this time?"

Cally sniffs, offended by his demeaning attitude, but nevertheless she obliges. "You, uh, reminded me of what happened." She shivers and wraps her arms around herself. Atlas has yet to remove his hand from her leg, his fingers still tucked behind her knee and thumb still resting beside her kneecap.

"Were you trying to forget about it?" He asks. Cally only nods. "Don't. Do not ever forget about it."

"Why?" Cally asks, astounded. "Why would I ever want to remember something like that?"

"Because there is something to be learned from every moment of our lives, even the bad ones. If you forget those moments, the things you might have learned from them may not be there to help you in the future." Atlas removes his grasp on her leg and instead reaches for their small bucket of rainwater. He pours a small amount over the injury, washing away the sting of the saltwater and the remaining blood along with it.

Once finished, he is disturbed to find her still silently crying. Normally, he would tune out her sniffles and ignore the scent of salty tears, yet this time he finds he cannot.

"Sing."

"W-what?" Cally asks, swiping at her nose once more.

"Sing," Atlas repeats. "It has helped you stop crying before."

"What--"

"You are so forgetful," Atlas mutters. "When you were in the cave, you sang once about a boy named Thomas or something. The singing made you stop crying," he explains.

"Do," a hiccup. "Do you mean Titus?"

"Yes, that was it."

"You were there," she whispers. Thinking back to when she had called to him in the cave those many weeks ago. He had not come at her calling, and so she sang to cheer herself up.

"You called me, hadn't you?" He asks.

Cally pulls her knees up to her chest, twisting her fingers together. The whole thing is rather embarrassing looking back on it now. "Why didn't you show yourself to me, then?" She asks, her crying turning into only small tears.

"You were in no danger, so I didn't see the point of making you aware of my presence."

Cally frowns. "Well, I wish you would have. I hadn't meant to sing in front of anyone."

Atlas doesn't respond. He does this sometimes whenever he wants the conversation to end. Most of the time, Cally gets frustrated with his lack of responses, but this time she is rather tired of talking herself.

Atlas leaves the tent soon thereafter, returning with the meal he had caught her. Whilst she cleans and cooks it (as he had taught her to do by this time), Atlas retrieves her clothes from the beach where the two had quite abandoned them in the hasty exit that evening.

After all is settled and Cally is back in her "Comfy clothes," as she calls them, Atlas stretches himself out on the sand, laying on his side supported by his elbow. Cally gets comfortable as well, crossing her legs beneath her and watching the flames. It is silent for a long while, so long that Cally is about to move to her side of the fire to sleep when Atlas suddenly speaks.

"I thought you were going to sing."

Cally laughs tiredly as she leans back on her hands. She looks down at the black mess of curls beside her, the sudden desire to touch them making her fingers twitch, though she refrains from doing so.

"You laugh, though I am quite serious, my dear human."

"I don't much care for singing to an audience," Cally explains. "I have only ever sung in front of my brother, and an eight year old isn't very judging."

Atlas chuckles quietly. "The admiration he has for his sister may also contribute to that."

"Exactly," Cally smiles.

"So will you sing, then?" Atlas asks quietly, dark eyes lifting to meet hers.

Cally rolls her eyes. "I thought we had already established that I only sing for eight-year-olds who admire me?"

"I may not be of eight years, but I do admire you," Atlas speaks honestly in his low, masculine voice.

Cally blushes the brightest red, ducking her head as her shoulders raise instinctively. "Why do you want me to sing so badly?"

"Is it a crime in your world to ask one you admire to sing?" Atlas asks plainly, eyes still boring up at her.

Cally would ask him why he admired her, but she felt it too vain a question. Instead, she answers him: "No."

"Then sing for me, Calliope."

Cally is more nervous than she has ever been when singing. It used to always be something she did to relax or be at peace, but now it felt more intimate than that.

In a way--a silly way--it felt like Cally was showing a hidden part of herself to Atlas. Never before had she sung for anyone, but she was singing for him. That fact made the situation so much more significant.

Cally chose a different song than what she sang before in the cave, a sweeter song that was more solemn. She began softly, praying she had started in the right key. Her words were shaky at first until she became more comfortable and her voice grew stronger. The verses passed smoothly from her lips more perfect than she had ever sung them before.

Atlas laid down completely, just listening to the human's song with his eyes closed so as not to distract himself with sight. Her voice filled the small home with waves of beautiful sound, echoing sweetly in the comely space.

Soon she was finished, and Atlas lay silently next to her. Too tired to round the fire to her own place, Cally found herself lying where she was, her body opposite Atlas' with her head less than a foot away from his.

Sleep was quick to overtake them with no further words spoken.

# Chapter 23

------------------------------------------------

When Cally arose that next morning, she was surprised to find Atlas still there with her. She was even more surprised to find him still asleep. It was only when she saw no sunlight shone through into their small home that she realized it wasn't yet morning.

Cally rested quietly while she awaited sleep's return. It was hard to believe how much had happened in only a little less than a fortnight. Atlas is human now, she witnessed a plane crash, Atlas saved her from a horrible fate, and now he had agreed to take her home. It was quite a lot to take in in such a short time. More so was the fact the she had befriended the male creature. Although, friendship does not quite encompass their relationship, but it is the only way Cally knows how to describe it. Then there were the words he spoke only a few hours ago.

"...But I do admire you."

Cally is quite unsure as to what exactly he admires about her, and she was afraid to ask at the time. What had me meant by admire? He wouldn't admire just anyone--no, Atlas was not that kind of man.

In what ways did he admire her? Was he... Flirting? No, surely not. Did Atlas even know what flirting was?

He had asked her to sing to him, and oh how sweetly he had asked. His words stayed with her while she sang. The way his voice lowered and his eyes lit up with a smile, it nearly made her melt.

"Then sing for me, Calliope."

She sang, and how beautifully had she sung. It was like a poet finally having their muse, or an artist painting his most beloved sitter, she had someone not to sing to, but to sing for. Cally hadn't ever experienced that before.

As she lay pondering all these things, she hadn't expected Atlas to suddenly speak.

"What are you thinking about so intently?" He asks, making Cally jump. She hadn't even realized he was awake whilst she thought those vain things!

She focuses her vision above to see Atlas propped on an elbow and looking down at her quite curiously. Cally crosses her arms, frowning.

"What makes you say I was thinking intently?" She quarries.

"I've been staring at you like this for many minutes now and yet you still had yet to notice me," he answers, smiling cockily down at her.

"Do you know what flirting is?" She suddenly asks.

It isn't her question that surprises Atlas, but her reaction afterwards. The silly little human covered her face immediately thereafter and groaned loudly into her palms, a faint "I should not have said that," audible.

"No, I don't," he answers honestly. "Is it a human practice?"

"Yes," she replies. "But it isn't important."

Atlas hovers his head above hers, smiling down at the perplexing girl. "Oh, but I think it is," he presses.

Cally spreads her fingers to peek up at him through the gaps in her hands. She scowls. Atlas grins.

"Well, I'm not telling you," she states indignantly.

Atlas curls his legs beneath him, placing himself beside Cally who has since turned away from him and faced the fire. Atlas' curiosity begins to grow as Cally becomes more reluctant to tell him. She obviously finds the topic embarrassing and hadn't meant to tell him about it, but oh, how exciting must it be that it makes her cheeks so red!

"Come on," Atlas pulls on Cally's shoulder to get her to face him. "You have to tell me."

Cally giggles reluctantly as his fingers dig into the ticklish flesh beside her neck. "Atlas!" She whines and beats his hand away. "I'm not telling you, I just wanted to know if you had heard of it before."

"But I want to know!" He complains childishly, tapping his fingers over her neck and shoulder, searching to elicit the giggles he had with prior touches.

"Stop--fine! Stop it that t-tickles!" She laughs through her struggles. Atlas releases Cally to allow her to sit up. She mirrors his sitting style and shakes away the lingering feeling of being tickled.

Atlas tilts his head. "Tickles?"

"Fine. I will answer that one next but first you have to promise me something."

"Alright," Atlas says eagerly.

"Promise me you will answer any questions I ask you," she says, pointing at him for emphasis.

Atlas shrugs. "Okay."

Cally sighs, mentally preparing herself for the impending doom of this conversation. "Well, flirting is a thing that humans do when we, uh, like each other. Mostly young humans do it."

"What exactly do you mean by like?" Atlas questions slowly. He watches with a grin as the human's cheeks slowly turn red.

"Kind of, uh, when two people are... When they really like each other?" She says as though it were more of a question than an explanation.

"Have we flirted?" Atlas bluntly asks.

"What? N--actually, I don't know..." Her shoulders sink in embarrassment, her entire face a pool of red.

"You don't know? Explain it better and I'll tell you what I think," Atlas suggests.

Cally bites her lip, refusing to look at him. "Its what people do to try and get someone else to find them attractive," she mumbles so quietly he almost can't hear it.

Atlas bursts out in the loudest laughter Cally has ever heard him use. His shoulders shake and his eyes squint with the size of his smile. Cally crosses her arms indignantly, a frown pulling at her lips. She hadn't expected him to laugh at her.

"You humans actually do that?" He exclaims finally. "But that's pathetic! I've never had to convince any female I was attractive!" His laughs begin to quiet. "Oh, Calliope, I'd never flirt with anyone. No woman is worth the loss of my dignity."

Atlas hadn't noticed until now how quiet Cally had become. Her eyes were cast away from him, the rosy blush on her cheeks gone away to be replaced with a sour frown. He was quite perplexed by the girl's reaction and worked frantically to understand what had made her upset.

Meanwhile, Cally was quite disappointed with herself. Of course he wasn't flirting with her, and it was childish of her to think he ever would. Atlas was of an entirely different species from her own, much better looking, and more... experienced than she in the way of attraction.

It was her own young femininity that made her think in such a way, and for that she was ashamed, but she couldn't much help it either. Though he had done horrible things in the past, he had also done so much to redeem himself since then, even risking his life to save her.

Atlas was something entirely new to Cally--mysterious, handsome, dangerous--something no one else would ever compare to. It was naive, yes, but no man had ever shown Cally any interest at all and to think that maybe Atlas would think of her as more...

"Was it something I said?" Atlas questions through a sigh of exasperation. Sometimes the little human's emotions were too much for him to handle.

Cally smiles sadly. "No. It's just my crazy imagination."

"What were you imagining?" He asks tentatively. Atlas decided he didn't like whatever it was she had imagined. It made her features crumble and her shoulders droop as though she were wilting. The look was altogether horrid on the chipper young girl.

"Nothing," she replies. "And I'd prefer if you wouldn't pry this time."

"I understand," he murmurs. Even though she says it was her imagination, Atlas can't help feeling like it was his fault.

Atlas stayed awake long after that. He watched the girl sleep fitfully--on her side of the fire. She never even looked at him after their short conversation and her distancing of herself from him only heightened his frustration. Perhaps she would sleep off this strange mood and if she didn't, well, he wasn't sure what he would do. All Atlas knew was he couldn't let her stay distressed like this.

He had promised to protect the girl and take her home, but it seems like the promise is becoming so much more than that.

# Chapter 24

When Cally awoke that morning, Atlas was gone. She hadn't realized it before, but she knew it now. Calliope missed his presence and that scared her more than anything she had ever encountered. She always wondered where he was when he hadn't been with her, and at the time she had thought that to be simple curiosity, but last night's events proved to be rather enlightening.

She wasn't the only one to find enlightenment that night. Atlas stormed from the tent as soon as the sun rose that morning. He had never protected anyone before, never spent time with anyone, never grown to care for another, but he had now.

He has protected Calliope, provided for her, learned of her culture and people, and now he... he cares. And so he was paying the price. He had wounded his little human in some way, therefore he would do everything in his power to fix it. The time he had with her was limited and he couldn't afford to lose the little trust she had in him.

When he arrived back on the beach that morning, he was soaking wet but very proud of himself. He caught a large fish that was a delicacy to his people and scavenged fruit from a neighboring uninhabited island, which was in his mind, the most perfect meal.

When he returned to the tent, she was gone, and for that he was thankful. She was most likely bathing and the girl was always happy after a bath. In the meantime, he set about preparing the fish and fruit. He cooked the meat just like he had seen her do many times before and sliced the orangish fruit, removing the nut.

He couldn't help wondering about the humans and the kinds of relationships they shared. Cally had told him all sorts of things and he wondered how he felt about Cally in human terms. He thought about married people and how she explained their love for each other. They pledged themselves to each other for their length of life on earth.

Did he.. did he love Calliope like she said spouses did? He really wasn't sure. To be fair, Atlas didn't really know what love like that was supposed to feel like. Humans accepted only one lover and at first he thought that was silly, but did he know anyone else like Cally? Did he know any other female who had her smile, her aspirations, her little human legs?

He didn't. To Atlas, there was only one Cally--one Cally just for him.

By the time all was finished, Atlas was quite proud. Already he knew exactly how she would react with her bashful smile, blushing cheeks and kind words. Yes, this would certainly fix whatever wrong he had done to her.

When Cally returned after her morning wash, she was surprised to see Atlas waiting for her with fish already cooked and sliced mango fully prepared for her to eat.

Cally had decided during her time alone that it would be best if she just kept her distance from Atlas, but how hard that was to do! All of this he had done for her when she hadn't asked him to, and she could see the expectancy in his gaze. He wanted her to like what he had done. It was not rocket science to figure that out.

She accepted the food with a smalls smile, one she was reluctant to show, and a whispered thank you.

She ate in silence, suffocating, dooming silence that had Atlas wanting to throw something. Oh, how very wrong he was! She must have found whatever injury he had caused utterly despicable! Cally had asked him not to pry but it was killing him not knowing how to fix his mistake.

As soon as she had finished, Atlas stormed out of the tent. If that wasn't enough, then he could do better. In all his time beneath the sea, he had seen many beautiful things. Countless creatures and plants existed on the ocean floor, hidden in reefs that were simply too beautiful to imagine if you'd never seen then before.

Atlas never much cared about these things, but now that he knew someone who would appreciate them, he did. It didn't take him long to find what he was looking for, and then he was swimming back to the surface. He set aside the small treasure then quickly set about searching the chest for the 'soap' Cally had shown him.

At the time, he hadn't noticed his attachment for the girl and therefore never used the product she so highly praised, but now he did. Atlas was not exactly sure how to use the soap, but he eventually managed. He wasn't sure that Cally would notice his new scent, but it was worth a try.

As he walked back to their small home, he found her sitting quietly on the rocks overlooking the sea. He took the tiny object that was to be Cally's gift and placed it in one of the pockets in his 'shorts.' He hadn't before realized how handy the pockets were until now. Atlas then climbed up the large rock to Cally's spot.

As he sat tentatively beside her, the only acknowledgement he received was a small, barely there smile. It was nothing compared to her usual hello and far from the jubilant smiled he longed to see.

Atlas said nothing to her. Instead, he only took the small gift from his pocket and held it out to her. He at first kept his gaze away from her, however his eyes quickly snapped to hers when he felt her hands around his.

"Atlas, is that... a pearl?" She asks, her hands pulling his palm which holds the white orb closer to her.

"Is that what your people call it?"

"Yes. Is it real, like, a real pearl?" She asks. "Are you going to keep it?"

Atlas frowns, shaking his head. "No, I'm giving it to you."

"Oh," she whispers softly, eyes falling away from his.

Atlas stiffens, fisting his hand tightly around the pearl and bring it to his lap. "You don't want it," he says, his words tight and controlled.

"What? No, I didn't say that--"

"You didn't have to!" He spits, standing to his feet and preparing to throw the innocent pearl.

Cally stands as well, grasping his arm as he rears back. "Please, I'm sorry Atlas. You just don't understand!"

"Of course I don't! He exclaims, obsidian eyes bearing down on hers. "How can I when you refuse to tell me how I've wronged you?"

Cally frowns pityingly, stroking her fingers up and down his arm. Her words are shaky when she speaks. "Oh, Atlas you never did anything wrong."

Atlas faces her fully. "I didn't?" He asks.

Cally shakes her head. "Quite the opposite."

"I don't understand."

"You are too kind to me, Atlas. You have done horrible things and yet everyday you try to make up for that. Everyday you build me a way to get home. Everyday you provide for me. You keep me company, listen to whatever I ramble on about. You don't understand what that means to someone like me."

He grasps both her elbows, the pearl long since tucked away in his pocket. "Then help me understand, Calliope."

"I-I..." Cally trails off, more uncertain than she's ever been.

"Please," he murmurs. "I'm trying so hard."

"I'm sorry," she says. "I know this isn't fair to you."

Atlas' brows furrow. "What isn't fair. Please, Cally. Just tell me!"

"I really like you, Atlas--more than I should," she says with surprising evenness. "And that isn't fair because I know how different we are--how differently you feel about me." Atlas shakes his head fervently but she continues: "I'm sorry I'm telling you this because I don't want you to feel like it's your fault I feel this way."

She loves me. Atlas can hardly contain the ecstatic smile that overcomes his face. "My little human. Are we really so different? And if we are, I don't care." He pulls her closer, his nose just inches above hers. "I love you," he says, not once hesitating.

Cally's face falls. "Atlas you don't know what--"

"No, I don't know what love is," he says. "But I like calling how I feel about you love."

"Atlas," she whispers sorrowfully. "I'm not going to be staying here."

"I know," he whispers back.

"You don't get it," she whimpers. "My heart is too soft--too fragile. I love too much and too easily."

"I know," he says again. "I see it everyday. I see it in the way you smile at me, when you help me, and when you talk to me, because it takes someone with a soft heart to show that much kindness to someone like me."

Cally's eyes glisten as she stares up at him. She can't find any words to speak, so she let's him continue.

"You say you aren't going to be here long, which is why I can't let this time with you go. I will live a very long life, Calliope, but to spend at least this small amount of it with you will last me until long after you have gone."

He reaches his hand up to her face, rough fingers delicately spreading over the expanse of her cheek and jaw. Cally's eyes flit all around his face, soaking in the sincerity of his words.

"Please," he murmurs. "Please, let me love you." His dark eyes search hers for any kind of answer, lips quivering. "Please."

Cally responded in a different way than he expected. Her eyelids fluttered shut, her hands pulling him down by the shoulders as she reached up on her tip toes. And then, in the lightest touch Atlas had ever felt, her lips pressed against his.

# Chapter 25

Atlas has felt the pleasure of a woman many times before. He has given in to fleshly desires, become drunk on male satisfaction, but never has he felt the way he does now. In this moment, with this woman, he is experiencing more than he ever thought possible.

As Calliope stood so close to him, her hands tugging lightly at his shoulders with her lips... Her lips pressing so tentatively--so uncertain--against his own, he knew that the passion he felt now was only a drop of what their love had to offer.

Cally slowly releases him, her arms falling back to her sides, heels returning to the ground. She ducks her head away from his gaze. He hadn't kissed her back. Cally suddenly wondered if maybe she misunderstood but that only lasted for a moment.

Atlas caught her fast, using both arms to pull her flush against him. She was shocked for just a moment before Atlas' mouth was on hers. He was not done yet. His lips move feverishly against Cally's, willing her to return the passion he was giving her. And, eventually, she did, her pink lips moving tenderly with his. His hands cupped her jaw, angling her head to his liking. Slowly, with much hesitation, her hands rested against his chest.

Atlas only released her when she pushed at his shoulders, a squeak sounding at the back of her throat. He pulled back very reluctantly, eyes meeting her own worriedly as she gasps for air.

"Are you alright?" He asks with concern, stroking her cheek before resting his hand on her waist.

She nods, laughing. "I need air, in case you forgot."

He had.

"I'm sorry," he says, smiling now. "In my defense, I was quite distracted."

Cally just giggled quietly, falling against his chest and wrapping her arms around his middle. Atlas was quite disappointed that their kissing was over, as he surely would have liked to continue, but having her resting calmly against him he found was just as satisfying.

He rubbed his hands up and down her back, massaging little circles. Atlas bowed his head and pressed a kiss onto her crown, his nose burrowing into her sweet smelling hair. He felt her head nod as she snuggled into his chest, ear against his heartbeat, and Atlas found it the most comfortable feeling in the world.

"The mango was delicious," Cally voices later that evening as they sat by the fire.

"The what?"

"The fruit. It is called a mango. It is also my favorite fruit."

"Your favorite?" He asks. "I'm glad."

It is silent for quite a while after that. Cally sits with her legs curled beneath her, facing the flames with her right knee just barely brushing Atlas' arm as he lounges beside her.

She glances at Atlas to see him already staring in her direction, gaze lazily curious.

"What are you looking at?" She asks, following his line of sight to somewhere around crossed legs.

"Your legs," he says simply.

"Okay..?" She says, drawing out the word.

"Why?" He asks, eyes glancing to meet her own. "Does it bother you?"

"No, it's just strange is all."

"Not to me," he replies. "What's strange is getting to see legs so close."

Cally giggles. "What? Have you not seen them this close before? You touched them last night," She quarries, watching a disgruntled frown fill his features.

"It is still new to me even so. It's not like you didn't stare at me when I was in my true form," Atlas grumps.

She slaps his shoulder. "I didn't even know you existed before then, of course I did! I also had to keep an eye on you, the way you snuck around."

Atlas smiles, though there is pain hidden in his gaze. "You were afraid."

Cally nods solemnly. "I was."

"If I..." Atlas swallows thickly. "When I go back to being what I truly am, will you be afraid of me again?"

Cally reaches for his hand, tenderly spreading her fingers across his knuckles. "No."

He stays still beneath her touch. "No?"

"No." She sighs. "I know you now. You are my Atlas and you would never harm me," she turns to him, grinning. "You told me so yourself."

Atlas smiles back, lifting her hand to press a kiss to her fingers. Of course, he didn't realize that was a gentlemanly action. He only knew the action felt right--conveyed his attentive loyalty to her.

Cally blushes, tugging her hand away from his as her palms grew sweaty. Atlas frowns at her hasty retreat, pushing himself into a seated position to scrutinize the bashful girl.

"Please don't tell me this is one of those silly human traditions," Atlas whines.

Cally rolls her shoulders, easing the redness from her cheeks. "What do you mean?"

"Am I not allowed to hold your hand, kiss your palm?" He asks, sorrowful horror filling his exotic features. "Do humans not allow such things in these relationships?"

"What? No!" Cally corrects. "No, I just... You make me nervous is all." She shrugs almost shamefully.

Atlas' jaw clenches. He shuffles away from her and places his arms over his knees. Nervous... Afraid. For Atlas, that hurt more than it would most people. Just when he thought he had won her favour...

"I understand," he replies, voice raw and expression that of stone.

"I'm sorry, this is all just so new to me," Cally rambles, completely unaware of Atlas' internal conflict. "I've never had a boyfriend before and I-I..."

"What are you talking about?" Voices Atlas.

Cally wraps her arms tightly around herself, biting her lip anxiously. "I don't know!"

Her gaze shifts to his, eyes full of uncertainty, fire light flickering over tanned cheeks. Atlas admires the woman before him, cursing himself for becoming so attached.

"You don't have to lie," he says plainly, the poor boy not understanding her discomfort. "If you are afraid of me still, just say so."

"No, that's not--ugh!" Cally groans behind her hands. "Not that kind of afraid."

Atlas wants to go to her, massage her shoulders and soothe her anxiety, but if she doesn't want to be touched, then fine! He won't touch her.

"Explain."

Cally slowly raises her gaze to meet Atlas' expectant eyes. She chews on the inside of her cheek anxiously, taking a deep breath.

"No boys have ever touched me like I've allowed you to, Atlas."

Said male forces down his inner triumph and instead schools his features to appear passive. "So?"

Cally shakes her head. "Why do you always seem to put me on the spot like this?" She questions more to herself. She sighs heavily. "Do you not have any idea how I feel?"

"No."

"Look at it this way: You have uh," she swallows. "Been with women before, but I... I'm completely out of my comfort zone here."

Atlas tilts his head, eyes squinting with his lips twitching up at the corners. Ah, now he understands. "I scare you in a sexual way."

Cally's mouth drops open in horror, cheeks flaming with a new rush of blood. At this point, she should have expected his bluntness. "No! That's not--"

Atlas cuts her off with a low, rumbling laugh from deep in his chest, though he sobers quickly. He looks at her with more adoration than Cally was prepared for, his smile not mocking, but earnest. "You are the most innocent little creature I have ever seen."

Cally doesn't respond, instead watching Atlas carefully as he moves closer to her once more. He moves close enough for his knees to touch hers, his longer torso allowing him to look down on her. His hand reaches for her cheek, moving her eyes to meet his.

He smiles not with ill intent nor amusement, but with kindness, love, and fear of his own. "I swore I would protect you and... And if that includes protection from myself as well, then I will do it."

Cally swallows thickly. Of all the things she had expected him to say, it was not this. "It's okay," she says quietly. "I'll be okay."

"Are you sure?"

Cally nods.

"Can I kiss you now?"

Cally nods again.

She closes her eyes, waiting for her creature's lips. She sat motionless with her lips slightly parted. As she sensed him moving closer, she was prepared for his mouth to connect with her own, but that isn't quite what happened.

Breath, warm and light breezes across her collarbones. A hand comes to rest lightly on her hip sending both excitement and trepidation to race up her spine. A nose gently nods against her own and just as she thought he would kiss her, he disappears.

Cally almost flinched as warm lips are suddenly at her jaw. The touch is brief, but returns again in a different place, this time just below her ear. Again, further down her neck. Fingers thread through the hair at the back of her neck, his large palm warm at the base of her skull.

He pulls gently, urging her chin up. She accommodates, soon feeling his lips on the column of her neck once, twice, three times. A fourth, this time longer, deeper. Her breath hitches, eyes still squeezing tightly shut.

The hand on her neck massages gently, his breath warm in her ear as he whispers: "Relax. I've got you."

Cally nods, holding on to Atlas as he descends on her collarbones. Warm mouth, lips soft and parted. The languid nipping of teeth and hot breath. Tongue tastes skin and hands grip tighter. Fingertips smooth across the flesh of her stomach, thumbs coming to rest on her lower ribcage. He pulls her ever closer.

It is in this moment that Cally puts all of her trust in Atlas. He had claws, but they never once pierced her skin; she only felt the soft pads of his fingers as they spread wantonly across her skin. His fangs never punctured the vulnerable flesh of her neck. They stayed tucked away with warm lips in their place.

Hands were used to soothe and draw pleasure rather than fear and blood. He kissed her skin when he had the chance to tear it apart. Atlas could have done a number of horrible things to her, but instead he chose to give the girl all the love he knew how to share.

"Atlas?" she whispers.

"Calliope?" He murmurs back.

"I love you."

# Chapter 26

<hr>

Cally's eyes open blearily, the comfort of a restful sleep still clinging to her heavy eyelids. She stretches her stiff limbs, not surprised to see Atlas not in his usual space. She is surprised, however, by the tightening of an arm around her middle.

She flops around ungracefully to face the still sleeping male, or at least he would have liked her to think he was still asleep.

Cally flicks his ear. "Atlas! I know you're awake. What do you think you're doing?"

"Sleeping?" He mumbles groggily. "What else would I be doing?"

Cally huffs indignantly. "I can see that, but why are you sleeping here?"

Atlas wiggles down to pull her closer, tangling his legs with hers and tucking his head beneath her chin. "Why not here? I can kiss you and hold you and touch you. Can I not lie next to you as we sleep?"

Cally wasn't quite sure what to say to that. In truth, he was right. Over the past many days, the two had spent almost every waking moment together. What was really so bad about sleeping next to him?

Atlas smiles triumphantly as he feels her fingers begin to play with the hair at the base of his neck. His eyes close lightly, lashes fluttering against his cheeks. He presses a tender kiss to her collarbone, tempted to nip at the supple flesh, though he refrains.

"We need to get up soon," she says after a while.

"Or maybe not," Atlas replies. "I find I am very content here."

"I know," she sighs. "But we need to eat and the tent needs some repairs."

Atlas kisses her neck again. "It can wait."

Cally giggles quietly, her voice trickling through the early morning air. His hair tickles the underside of her chin. "Yeah but--"

Atlas pushes the girl onto her back, rolling on top of her. "No," he says, trying to remain serious but the smile is bright in his eyes.

Cally half-heartedly pushes at his chest. "C'mon, Atlas. I need a bath."

Atlas' nose dives behind her ear, his breath tickling her neck and making her giggle. "Nah, you smell fine to me."

"I don't care what you think," she says bravely. "I want a bath, so I am going to get one."

"Not if I don't let you," he counters, pinning her legs and reaching for her wrists. Before he can grab hold of her hands, she reaches up and pulls his lips down to meet her. She grips him firmly by the neck, her lips moving roughly against his.

Atlas is quick and eager to respond, tugging and nipping at her lips, his tongue searching for a way to meet hers. He barely registers that she flips them back over, only that he likes the weight of her body on his. His breath comes fast as he kisses her more passionately, his hands beginning to wander.

Just before he can take hold of her hips, he finds them disappearing completely. His eyes fly open to see Cally pushing herself off of him, her wicked smirk taunting him.

"Calliope!"

She just laughs, dodging his hands that reach for her ankles as she prances away. He slumps back on the ground as the last of her blonde hair passes out of sight, the girl muttering something about toothpaste as she leaves.

Atlas slaps his palm on his forehead, the lingering softness of her lips leaving him wanton for more.

"Weak," he mutters.

"A ukulele?"

"Yeah, it's an instrument," Cally answers.

"That tells me nothing," he deadpans.

"It makes music," she explains. "It has four strings that attach to a hollowed wooden frame and when you stroke the strings it makes music."

"And you have one?" He asks, fingers slipping into her hair. He really isn't paying attention, more focused on playing with her hair, but he likes listening to her voice.

"Yeah. I play it all the time. I... I wish you could hear it," Cally mumbles slowly, hollow.

Atlas pauses. He knew what she was thinking by her sullen words. He didn't have the courage to address what they were both thinking, so he didn't. "Your voice is music enough," he said at last.

Cally blushes bashfully. She ducks her head, blonde hair tugged away from his lingering fingertips. "You make me sound so much better than I actually am."

"Hmm," Atlas hums, stretching himself out and resting his head on her lap. "Better than you think you are is more correct."

His onyx eyes stare up at her as though she were perfection itself; it almost made it hard for her to keep eye contact. Cally smiles, brushing his bangs away from his eyes. "Whatever," she sighs. "You are beautiful, you know that?" She traces her fingertips over his cheeks, smoothing over his eyebrows and letting them linger over his lips.

"Yes," he replies with arrogant seriousness. "But it means so much more hearing you say it."

Cally flicks his nose. "Quit being so egoistic! I was trying to complement you."

Atlas smirks. "Complement accepted."

Cally just laughs, the two lapsing into a comfortable silence. No speaking was done, only the occasional sigh and the passing of content smiles. Hands would languidly drift over skin, fingers tiptoeing across fair complexions leaving tingles in their wake. Eyes would cast affectionate glances, shy smiles sharing the kind of thoughts only lovers understood.

The waves crashed smoothly in the background, gulls calling overhead. Sunlight streaks through golden hair, alighting on rosy cheeks to create a sight much like that of an angel--an angel to Atlas at least.

"Sing."

It was neither a question nor a command, but it was answered either way. Atlas' eyes closed as the voice of his love floated about him. The sound of her song was felt deep in his chest, saturating his soul with the warmth and light that seemed to always encase her.

Took my breath from my open mouthNever know how it broke me downI went in circles somewhere elseShook the best when your love was homeStoring up on your summer glowYou went in search of someone elseAnd I hear your ship is comin' inYour tears a sea for me to swimAnd I hear a storm is comin' inMy dear, is it all we've ever been?

She sang softly, her voice a musical whisper in the breeze. Her eyes closed as she was swept away in the moment. Atlas was full of contented sighs, his eyes opening every so often to see his lover's face. Lashes fluttered against her rosy cheeks, luscious lips shaping to form the words of the poetry she sang. He watched the blush rise up her neck as she caught him staring, but she didn't look away. She stared back at him with so much affection and love, that Atlas wondered if her expression was a mirror of his own.

Anchor up to me, love

Anchor up to me, love

Anchor up to me, love

Oh, anchor up to me, my love, my love

My love.

"I love you so much that I think my love for you has become a part of me. I think that if I didn't love you, a part of me would be missing," Calliope says at the end of her song.

Atlas raises her hand to his cheek, pressing her warm palm to his jaw. His eyes conveyed exactly the same as she said, only his gaze was enough to express it. Her thumb lovingly caressed his cheek and Atlas turned his head to press a lingering kiss to the inside of her hand.

"Say it again," he murmurs, eyes earnest and searching. "Tell me you love me," while we are still together.

"I love you."

"I will never tire of hearing you say that," Atlas whispers. "Never."

"And I will never tire of saying it," she whispers back, bending down to kiss him slowly, passionately.

Atlas would always love her. As long as he lived, he would never stop caring, protecting, loving her. He would love her even when she was no longer there to hear him say it. He would scream it at the top of his lungs even if the sound would never reach her ears because Atlas loved Calliope, and to him that was all that mattered.

"I love you so much," he said into her ear. He kissed her cheek softly and just revelled in having her so close. He didn't need her any closer than they were, as having her love was more than enough to satiate him.

As the sun steadily fell and darkness crept across the sky, as the breeze turned cool and the gulls grew silent, the couple strode back to their home by the shore. As they went, they passed the little raft that was built to take Cally home. When it was first constructed, Cally was ecstatic, but now...

Now the sight of the little boat saddened her more than she ever could have thought. She pulled her gaze away and leaned closer to Atlas, clutching his arm as though he would float away.

I'm sorry if you find this chapter boring. The two are falling hopelessly in love and I don't think there needs to be any action or drama for that to happen.

I have said this before, but I will say it again. I am so in awe of Atlas and Calliope and their love that I feel like a dirty puddle in comparison.

# Chapter 27

Cally's fingers lace through Atlas's. Her fingers are soft and pliable against his rough callouses and once--sometimes twice--broken knuckles. Her thumb gently caresses the back of his palm, raising his hand to her lips.

She kisses his fingers sweetly then pulls his hand to her chest, hugging it close to her as a child would its doll. Atlas feels the beat of her heart against his palm, the steady thump a sound he enjoys even more than her singing. The rhythm is slow and relaxed, openly showing how comfortable she is with him. He remembers when her heart rate would skyrocket whenever she was in his presence, but now it seems to do just the opposite. That isn't to say he can't still make it race, though in a far different way.

Atlas detangles his other hand from her hair and sweeps her blonde tresses over her shoulder, exposing her back and neck to him. His lips soon find the base of her neck, pressing a lingering kiss to her sensitive skin. Cally shivers. Atlas smiles.

"If you hold my hand captive, it makes brushing your hair much more difficult," he murmurs against her skin.

Cally leans back into his chest, her head tilting to gaze up at him serenely. She smiles languidly, her eyes half-lidded. "I couldn't help it."

Atlas bows his head, brushing his cheek against hers. "I suppose I don't either, as long as I get to hold you like this."

Cally looks down with a blush, seeing his legs on either side of her with his chest pressed flush against her back. She had never sat with another boy like this, but she couldn't bring herself to care. This was Atlas--her Atlas.

Cally relaxes completely, her head falling to the side to accommodate Atlas as he peppers kisses all across her neck. Down the side of her jaw, on the space between her neck and shoulders, even in the hollows of her collarbones.

"Atlas?" She suddenly asks. The boy doesn't stop, just letting out a "Hm?" between kisses. "Where are your claws?"

Atlas sighs, nipping her skin gently with his teeth as a reluctant goodbye from her intoxicating flesh before raising his head back up. "What do you mean?"

"Well, I've seen you use them in your human form before, but they aren't here now," she says, touching her fingertip over his blunt human nails.

"I use them when I need them," he says. "They are still a part of me no matter which form I reside in. It's how I can still breathe underwater also."

Cally watches fascinatedly as sharp, black claws push through his nail beds. She runs her own hands over his, marvelling at the strange sight. Soon enough, his hands return to normal.

"Does it hurt?" She asks, massaging his knuckles.

"Only like a small sting," he explains. "Nothing to be concerned about." He sighs, nuzzling his nose into her freshly washed hair. "As much as I love this, we need to brush your hair before it gets any worse."

Cally pouts, holding his arm tighter. "My hair is fine."

Atlas laughs quietly. "You say that until yesterday repeats itself."

Cally frowns, remembering trying to detangle the matted mess while Atlas was gone. "Ugh, fine, but be quick."

Atlas obliges, pulling his hand from her grasp and placing one last, lingering kiss behind her neck. His hands work deftly as he moves the comb through her blonde locks. Atlas loves her hair. The golden strands look so delicate in his rough hands. The boy suddenly feels inferior to her pure nature.

"How old are you, Atlas?" Cally asks a few minutes later.

"Twenty-two Tides."

"So twenty-two years?" Cally guesses. She hadn't really thought about his age before, but twenty-two was close to what she had already assumed.

"I suppose," he replies. "How old are you?"

"I'm eighteen," she says happily.

"You are younger than I thought," Atlas admits. "But then again, it's not like I've ever had to guess a woman's age before."

Cally shrugs, wincing as he pulls on a particular knot. "I'll take that as a compliment. Most people always think I'm younger than my actual age."

"Does that bother you?"

Cally sighs. "Well, not anymore. I guess now I don't really care. We are all going to lose our youth one day, so what we think of ourselves now doesn't really matter."

Atlas nods in agreement. "But you will be no less beautiful in my eyes when that time comes."

Cally can't help the smile that splits her cheeks.

The sun is warm on Cally's back.

The golden rays coat her skin and make her hair glow an angelic color. Though the heat of the sun is warm and pleasurable on her skin, they are nothing compared to the touch of Atlas' fingertips over her bare skin. They rise from the curve of her waist, gliding beneath her shirt and tenderly caressing her spine.

Her elbows rest on the sand beside his head, their gazes locked with affectionate eyes. Cally reaches her hand up to touch the side of his face, smiling as his nose turns into her palm. She presses a kiss beneath his jaw, her eyes closing as his hand pulls her chin up to align their lips.

Atlas will never tire of feeling her skin, of tasting her lips, or of hearing her sweet voice in his ear as she murmurs her love between kisses. He will never forget the way her eyes glow brighter when the sun touches them, or the way her hands play with his hair, or how her body trembles when their kisses turn passionate.

For Atlas, physical release had always been for personal gain. He got what he wanted while whatever female approached him got what she wanted. It was a symbiotic relationship of equal, selfish gain. But now... everything was about her.

Atlas no longer wanted to please himself, he wanted to please Cally. He wanted to give her his love, his passion, his pleasure. He found that pleasing her was far more significant than using her for his own selfish desires. With that came restraint and control, but all of it was worth it as long as she was comfortable and happy.

All of it was worth it.

"Tell me about your world," Atlas says as he pulls away to gaze at her once more.

"There is a lot to tell," Cally replies, resting her chin on his chest. "Is there anything in particular that you would like to know?"

Atlas shrugs, wrapping an arm around her shoulders. "What do humans do with their lives, I guess? My people just eat, mate, and survive."

Cally giggles quietly, the little rumbles felt against Atlas' chest. "Ugh, where to begin? Well, as kids we go to school--it's where we learn about things from adults. After that, some of us do more school."

"Will you be one of those?" Atlas asks.

"I hope so," she says. "This kind of schooling is much harder. Whatever craft we decide to learn about is how we make money later on, so it is very hard picking out what to study."

"Have you decided?" Atlas asks as he presses a kiss to her temple.

"I... haven't, actually. I have been thinking about being a school teacher, but that just doesn't feel like the right thing for me."

"You would do wonderful working with children," Atlas says. He can imagine her surrounded by small humans, her voice as she taught them whatever it is humans teach, even singing to them. It makes him realize how good of a mother she will be.

Cally smiles, resting her head on his shoulder. "I just... I feel like there is more I could with my life than just being a teacher. I mean, there is nothing more important than educating the next generation, but I don't think that's where I am supposed to be."

"Well, where do you think you are supposed to be?"

"I... I'm not quite sure yet."

Atlas kisses her forehead once more. "Whatever you decide upon, you will do a fantastic job."

Cally grins. "Who knew you could be so supportive?"

"Well, I wasn't supportive until I met someone worth supporting," Atlas murmurs in her ear.

The couple falls quiet as they watch the sun begin to set. Cally languidly traces patterns on his chest, her fingers leaving lingering tingles on his skin. He loves having her so relaxed with him, her body resting on top of his own with her eyes happy and lips smiling down at him. He wants to kiss her again.

"Where are you from?" Atlas suddenly asks.

Cally smiles thinking of her home so far away, the place she grew up and spent the entirety of her childhood. "A little town in a place called Michigan," she says. "It is thousands of miles away from here."

"How did you end up on the island, then?" He asks.

"We were on vacation here. Now that I am eighteen, my parents wanted to take me someplace special before I moved away. They thought the island would be a nice retreat."

Atlas stays quiet. He supposes he ruined that trip then. "What is your home like?" He questions, switching the direction of the conversation.

A heavy wave of nostalgia falls over Cally. She remembers everything about it, so she describes it to Atlas as best she can.

"It is warm there in the summer, but not nearly as warm as it is here. The winter is my favorite season up there, though. It gets really cold but there is so much snow. Have you seen snow before?"

Atlas shakes his head. "I cannot say that I have."

Cally's eyes light up as she begins to describe snow to him. "It is frozen rain, but not like ice. They are little tiny flakes of it, powdery and white. It falls from the sky slowly and you will never hear a silence more quiet than snow as it falls. It's a hassle sometimes, as it gets everywhere, but I still love it so much. The cold weather, snowy nights, hot chocolate... it's the most perfect time of the year. There is a hill behind my house that's super steep. My brother and I go sledding on it all the time. The neighbors would always come to our house to play on those days, and my mom would make soup and hot chocolate for all of us when we came inside.

"When I was little, before Ethan was born, we had one of the hugest snow storms I'd seen. The snow was so deep that it was taller than me! My dad and I went and dug in it for what seemed like days building tunnels and ditches and mini houses. It was the most fun I've ever had..." she trails off wistfully.

Atlas just rubbed his hands up and down her arm, nodding his head and kissing her cheek and jaw. He did listen, but his attention was more focused on how happy she was rather than the actual words she was saying. She loved her home, and so Atlas loved it too. It comforted him to know she was going back to a place she adored.

"Will you be safe there?" He asks quietly.

Cally's happy mood dampens. "Yes, I will."

Atlas pulls her tighter against him. "Good," he says. "I don't know what I would do if you wouldn't be. Are you... happy to be going home?"

Cally feels the sting of tears behind her eyes, a sudden realization flooding her mind. "I... I don't know."

Atlas stiffens, but he forces himself to stay relaxed. "You will be."

"Will I?" She whispers quietly, almost to herself.

"Yes," Atlas answers for her.

It is quite a moment before Cally speaks up, asking the question they both dreaded. "How much time do we have left?"

They hold each other closer. Atlas speaks slowly, his voice tight and words nearly choked. "A week at most."

# Chapter 28

Atlas' eyes trace every one of Cally's features, all the way to the smallest detail. A small, button nose splattered with freckles centered between high, smooth cheekbones. A few spots of acne are dotted on her cheeks, even some scars from previous ones, but Atlas doesn't mind that. They are a part of her just as much as the rest of her body.

More freckles are on her forehead--nine of them--just above her eyebrows. He finds the little speckles her most endearing feature. Dark lashes lay still on her cheeks, vivid grey eyes hidden beneath. Thin brows rest above them, wild an unkempt.

His hand delicately traces down her neck, stopping to rest at her collarbones. Her smooth skin feels like velvet beneath his fingertips. He runs his open palm over her shoulder and down her arm, threading his fingers with hers.

He lays himself gently next to her, pulling her close and resting her head against his chest. He should be asleep right now. Cally will be angry if she finds out he stayed awake again. But how could he? How could he sleep away the time he has with her?

He holds her as tightly as he can without waking her, wishing more than anything that they could just stay like this forever. He would hold her for an eternity if he could, just the two of them alone on this island. He wishes he could stay as a man. He wishes he could give her all the things she wants in life. He wishes he could give her a home, a life, children.

But he can't and that hurts worse than any pain he has ever had to endure. No matter how much she wishes to stay, he cannot give her what she wants--what she needs. Calliope deserves so much more than what he can offer.

More than anything, Atlas wanted to leave the tent and march out to the little raft he had built. He wanted to tear the thing to shreds, cast the pieces back into the sea, ensure that she would never leave him.

But what kind of man would that make him?

Who is he to take all that away from her? Calliope had a life waiting for her back home, a family to return to, a career to pursue. She has so much left to accomplish, and she can't possibly do that wasting away on an island.

She would soon hate Atlas, he knew that. It would never be fair to the girl to force her into staying, no matter how much she thought she wanted it. Her place was back home, among her people and very, very far from here.

Atlas' eyes began to sting. It was a foreign feeling, one he hardly recognized. Tears. After so many years of pushing away any emotions he every had, he had finally lost his control. He was crying. Atlas buried his face in her hair, suppressing his urge to sob. He wouldn't wake her. Not like this.

She has so much waiting for her, but what does he have? Nothing. Atlas has no family to return to, no life to await him, and no other possible chance of finding love. Before, he was completely content with his life, but now? Cally had opened his mind to so much more. She had told him of families, of husbands and wives, of education and culture and music. How could he possibly return to the sea when he knew what great wonders were truly out there?

But he must. His place is not among those who dwell on land. As much as he may want children, he would only want them to be Cally's children. He could never see himself with anyone but her. The human girl had taken a place in himself that no other could ever come close to filling. She would always be a part of him, and that is something he will always cling to.

Atlas tried to memorize every single part of her. Every tiny detail he focused in his memory because he wasn't sure what he would do if he ever forgot what she looked like. Small shoulders and delicate hands. A flat stomach and narrow hips. Short legs and adorable feet. She was just her. His beautiful Calliope.

His chest ached with the thought of losing her. He memorized everything about her because soon she would be gone and his memories would be the only place she could stay with him. It hurt so much.

Atlas soon felt warm fingers spreading across his cheeks, wiping away his tears. He opened his eyes to see his beautiful Calliope staring up at him, her delicate features morphed into an expression of the deepest sorrow.

"I know," is all she says before pulling him closer. The two hold each other so tightly it is almost hard to breathe.

"I don't want to be sad," Cally says as she gazes at the beautiful horizon over the sea. "I want to be happy in my last time with you, but I can't help it."

Dry tear stains marre her cheeks, her voice rough from crying. Atlas kisses both her cheeks. "Its okay to be sad."

"How long?"

"Tonight."

Fresh tears spring forth and Cally can't help the sob that chokes her throat. Atlas pulls her to his chest as her shoulders begin to shake. He told her it was okay to be sad, but damn if it doesn't hurt to see her like this.

"I'm not ready. Not yet, Atlas. Please not yet."

Atlas runs his hands in circles on her back. "I know it's hard, but you can't stay here. Look at us now, how I hold you in my arms and your legs are curled between mine. Look at my hands--hands that can't accidentally hurt you with claws. I won't stay like this forever. I can only be with you like you deserve once a year and slowly, that time will become less and less as I grow older."

"I wish it didn't have to be like this," she whispers against his skin.

"I know." Atlas raises her hand to press a kiss on the inside of her wrist. "You said before that I didn't know what love truly was, but I know now. I know that what I feel for you is an emotion that I can't quite fit into words. I love you in the most mundane ways, like how I love to see you lying beside me when I wake up in the morning or when you make that expression of thought whenever you think particularly hard about something and your nose scrunches and your eyebrow furrows to make the cutest dimple, but I also love you in the most poetic of ways. I love how your hair shimmers like gold in the sun, how your voice is the most beautiful thing I will ever hear, and how your touch is what I desire most often. I love the ways you kiss me. Sometimes it is a kiss full of passion and desire, other times it is simple and sweet, a quick peck to my cheek before going somewhere.

"I remember our first kiss, how you held me so hesitant, your lips pressed so lightly against mine. I won't ever forget your face after our second kiss, seeing you so out of breath with your lips swollen as a testament of the love I had shown you."

Cally sobs harder into his chest, knowing that no one could ever show her the love she is receiving now. She cups his cheek in her palm, her puffy eyes staring up into his dark obsidian ones. She uses her other hand to reach around his neck and pull his face down to hers.

Cally kisses him tenderly, but with much intent. Her lips move in a slow pace but they press firmly against his. She tries to show him as much love as she possibly can through her actions. Atlas tastes the salt of her tears but ignores it, instead focusing on returning her passion.

As she pulls away, her gaze meets his. He smiles slowly, sadly. "And that kind of kiss I love most of all."

"Please tell me we have more time," she pleads, hands moving desperately over his features, committing to memory every inch of his face through her hands.

Atlas shakes his head, hating what it does to her expression as it crumbles. "I can feel it. We don't have much time." He pulls her arm from around his neck, opening her palm. He reaches into his pocket before pulling out a small trinket Cally had very near forgotten about. "I want you to have this," he says, curling her hand around the small item.

Cally opens her hand to reveal the small pearl he had gifted to her only a few short weeks ago. Her fingers smooth over the small white orb with wonder and love. "It's beautiful. I... I wish I had something to give you."

Atlas brushes a small strand of hair away from her face, pulling her close to kiss her softly. "You have already given me everything I could have ever wanted."

Before Cally can respond, Atlas suddenly slumps over, a groan escaping his lips. "Atlas!" Cally exclaims, holding his head to her chest as he falls against her.

He looks up at her with torture written across his features, though not a torture of the physical kind.

"It's time."

Cally just nods, her lip wobbling, not trusting her voice. With great effort, she helps him stand. The sun steadily sets on the horizon as the two slowly make their way to the beach. Atlas stumbles time and time again as his legs cease to function.

Finally to where the waves lap against the shore, Atlas collapses to the ground. Cally kneels down beside him, her hands reaching to catch his head. He catches her wrists, pulling them away from him as he fixes her with his gaze.

"I don't want to hurt you," he says urgently as his body begins to writhe and shake.

Cally tears her hands from his and lays them delicately on either side of his face. She hovers her head over his, her tears dripping down onto his cheeks. "You won't hurt me," she whispers bravely.

Atlas just smiles a pained grin up at the courageous human girl he loves so much.

His legs kick and twitch, his hands digging into the sand to ground himself. Cally keeps her hands firmly on his cheeks, keeping his gaze on hers as she desperately tries to take his mind off the pain. Atlas cries out as claws suddenly burst through his fingertips, drawing blood this time as they become permanent.

Atlas' eyes squeeze shut in pain as he struggles to cope. "C-Cally," he says through gritted teeth.

Cally just nods, understanding, taking a deep breath before removing the last article of clothing from the lower part of his body. Her gaze returns to his once more. She whispers into his ears, voicing her love and affection to him as he once more becomes who he truly is.

Scales begin to rise along his thighs, his legs falling limp as they are soon covered and stretched to form a long, black tail. The last of the sun's light flashes on his scales, the shiny black alighting in emerald before the sun disappears along with the last traces of his humanity.

Cally rocks gently back and forth with Atlas' head in her lap. He lays against her silently, too weak to say anything. Cally curls herself around his head and shoulders. She clutches herself tightly to him, her head buried in his chest to hide her tear streaked face. Slowly, steadily, Atlas' arms find the strength to hold onto her as she cries.

Cally lies in the sand with her arms looped around Atlas, who lies with his fins in the waves and his arms clinging around the woman who is soon to be taken away from him.

# Chapter 29

------------------------------------------------------------

S teadily, the moon descends from the sky, the sun rising in its place. The tide recedes and the gulls fly up from their hideaways in the rocks. The breeze picks up its pace, blowing it's way down the beach and tickling the hairs at the base of Cally's neck.

Atlas brushes those strands away and rests his hand on the back of her head, his fingers occasionally dipping down to stroke her neck. Her thumbs stroke his cheeks, his eyebrows, his lips, fingertips affectionately tracing his every feature.

No tears were shed, as they had long since run out of those sometime during the night. They just stared at each other silently, kissing, touching, holding. Atlas and Cally only lay still, each basking in the presence of the other.

Their time together had run out and now this was all that they had left.

"I don't regret it," Cally whispers. "I knew it would hurt, but I don't regret it--I never will."

Atlas rests his forehead against hers. "Neither do I." Atlas pulled away from her, propping himself up on his elbows. He then spoke the words that neither of them ever wanted to hear. "We need to go."

He looks down at her lying in the sand, her eyes dark and hollow, skin pale. She looks dead. She gazes up at him with an expression so tragic he can barely stand to see it.

"I know."

Atlas is left on the shore as Cally goes alone back to their home. The little homemade tent blows gently in the early morning breeze. She pushes the flap aside to step in. She falls to her knees with a hand to her mouth as she can hardly contain her emotions.

The fire has gone cold, the coals long since cooled to an ashy grey. Across the fire from here is where she first sang to him; she remembers how the flames cast shadows over his angular cheekbones, the cheekbones she's kissed so many times.

Her hands press softly into the leaves where they laid together those few nights. She remembers how his skin felt warm under her cheek as she laid on his chest. It was only a few days ago when he surprised her by sneaking to her side, curling himself around her while she slept.

Even now Cally can picture the awe she saw in his eyes when she told him about her world, the interest in his voice as he asked question after question. There was still so much she hadn't told him--so much she wanted to show him.

Atlas clutched his chest as the sound of her sobs reached his ears. And here he was stuck, unable to reach her, unable to comfort her. He couldn't run to her and pull her into his arms.

Soon she returned carrying a shirt full of food for their journey. Her eyes were puffy, cheeks red. Atlas' heart broke. Cally walked silently to the raft and began dragging it to the water. She didn't speak, she could hardly look at him without crying again.

When she was close enough, Atlas took the other end. He swam out with the small raft to where it was about thigh-deep for Cally. When he turned to look back at her, she was still on the beach. Her back was to him, looking at the small island she had grown to love so much.

Cally turned to see Atlas watching her. She looked deeply into his eyes then slowly returned her gaze to the island. As she stood motionless on the shore, she wondered which way was home.

"Calliope," he says slowly. "Its time to go now."

The sun was hot on Cally's back. She sat with her feet dangling in the water to cool herself as Atlas swam. He looked so natural. The way his tail moved effortlessly in the water was purely hypnotic.

She was also surprised by the speed at which they moved. She wishes he were slower. They had already been on the open sea quite a few hours and by now the small island had completely disappeared. Atlas was beneath the water, so she couldn't talk to him. Instead, she just watched.

Cally looked up and almost gasped. There, on the horizon, was land. There was land, waiting for her with open arms and Cally couldn't bring herself to be happy. She focused her gaze back on the water, watching as it swept past her with the heavy strokes of Atlas' tail.

It wasn't long before Cally could see the definitive outline of the trees, though the white shore was still out of sight. "Atlas!" She suddenly called out. "Atlas!"

Atlas appeared before her, his hair wet and shoulders glistening. He just stared at her, gaze steady, waiting for her to speak.

"Take me back," she commands. "Bring us back to the island. Please, Atlas, take me home."

Atlas reaches for her hand, taking it into his and squeezing it tightly. He looks up at her, dark eyes steady on hers as he pleaded with her. "I am taking you home," he explains. "I am taking you to the home you need--where you will be loved and cherished and protected."

"But won't I have those same things if I stay with you? You have protected me before, you love me. Is that not good enough?"

"Cally--"

"No!" Cally shouts, pulling herself away from him. "I'm begging you, Atlas. Please, let me stay with you. It's all I want. Just please," her voice chokes on a hiccup as she pleads with him, her heart breaking as he remains emotionless. "Let me love you."

Let me love you.

Those were the same words he had said to her those short weeks ago. Oh, how badly he wanted to, how badly he wanted to take her back to the island and keep her there forever. But she deserves so much more.

He pulls her back down to him, his hands placed on either side of her head to hold her still. "Look at me," he says fiercely. "Tell me what you see."

"I see the man I love."

Atlas crumbles. "No, my love. Look at my hands. Do you see the claws? Look at my arms. Do you not see the fins and scales? I don't even have legs..."

"I don't care!" Cally exclaims. "I don't care what you look like."

"But you should. I can't give you what you deserve, Calliope. I can't give you a house, a career, my body, children."

Cally remains silent.

"You need those things--"

"No. I need you!"

"Stop!" Atlas shouts at her. His own eyes turn glassy when he sees tears begin to form in her eyes once more. "Stop," he whispers. "You think those things aren't important until you can no longer have them."

"But I don't care anymore. I will give it all up for you. I love you enough to do that, can't you see?"

"And I love you enough that I can't let you do that." Atlas swallows, forcing his voice not to shake. His thumbs stroke away her tears. "I love you so much that everytime I look at you I see the pain I could cause you. Don't you see? I wouldn't be able to live with myself knowing I took your entire life away from you."

"No--"

"Yes," he whispers. "Do you remember when you told me about school?" She nods. "You were glowing. You had no idea which direction you were going to go, but you were so excited no matter which way you chose.

"Do you remember telling me how you wanted to make a difference in the world? Your eyes lit up with so much ambition and you never looked more beautiful."

"Atlas, stop," she whispers, knowing he was getting to her.

"Do you remember telling me about the children you wanted?" Atlas continues with as much strength as he can muster. "Two boys and a baby girl."

Cally shakes her head, hands gripping his tighter.

"So you see then," Atlas says, shedding a tear of his own. "You see."

"But how can I do that without you?" She says miserably. "How can I do all of those things without you by my side?"

"Oh, my darling," he whispers. "I'll always be there."

Cally cries harder, resting her forehead against his. "I don't want to go."

"I know," he says. "I know." He pulls away, stroking her tear stained cheeks. He looks at the land looming ever closer, the tide steadily pulling them in. He rests his elbows on her knees, careful not to graze her skin with his claws, with his head in her lap. "Sing to me," he pleads. "Just one last time."

I wanna be aloneAlone with you, does that make sense?

She stops, a hiccup forcing her to go quiet. "I... I can't," she says.

"Shhh," he soothes. "Its okay."

I wanna steal your soulAnd hide you in my treasure chestI don't know what to doTo do with your kiss on my neckI don't know what feels trueBut this feels right so stay a secYeah, you feel right so stay a secAnd let me crawl inside your veinsI'll build a wall, give you a ball and chainIt's not like me to be so meanYou're all I wantedJust let me hold youLike a hostage

Her voice is wobbly and shaky like the first time he heard her voice. It makes him ache to know that he was the cause of this. Still, he is selfish enough to relish in the feel of her warm skin. He is addicted to her enough to make her sing more.

Gold on you fingertipsFingertips against my cheekGold leaf across your lipsKiss me until I can't speakGold chain beneath your shirtThe shirt that you let me wear homeGold's fake and real love hurtsAnd nothing hurts when I'm aloneWhen you're with me and we're aloneAnd let me crawl inside your veinsI'll build a wall, give you a ball and chainIt's not like me to be so meanYou're all I wantedJust let me hold youHold youLike a hostageLike a hostage

Cally can see the shore now. She can see the sandy white beach and the sea gulls as they fly past. She can see other humans on the beach. It surely won't be long now until she is spotted.

"Beautiful," Atlas murmurs. "So beautiful." She was finished and he couldn't stand it. He wanted to hear her sing over and over. He wanted her voice in his ear when he kissed her neck. He wanted the touch of her lips. He wanted to see her face every morning when he awoke, to see the sun shine in her golden hair and see the freckles on her cheeks alighted by the fire.

"Atlas," she whispers.

"Calliope."

"I love you."

The sound of an engine was heard, a small boat approaching from a distance. Atlas slid back into the water but Cally caught his hands. They looked at each other with so much love, and yet so much pain.

Atlas pulled her lips to his and kissed her with so much affection, so much pain, so much fear, so much love. Cally held him so tightly her hands shook. She is terrified of letting him go--she can't let him go.

"I love you, Calliope. So much, so much." His lips were on her cheek, her neck, her lips, her forehead. His hands were everywhere, touching her cheeks, cupping her neck, holding her arms. "Don't you ever forget that."

"I won't," she swore. "I will always love you."

"Hey! Miss!" Cally whipped around to see the boat was only a few meters away, preparing to retrieve her.

She turns to Atlas to see him smile once more. He kisses her, his lips lingering as he struggles to find the will to pull away. His lips leave hers for the last time, hands reaching to wipe her cheeks. He holds her hand as he sinks back into the sea, his gaze never leaving hers as slowly, with so much pain it nearly kills him, Atlas lets her go.

"I love you."

The last she sees of him is his long, black tail that glints in the sun before disappearing beneath the waves.

"I love you," she whispers back to the sea.

# Chapter 30

The snow falls steadily outside Cally's bedroom window. The flakes swirl as they fall, accumulating on the frozen earth. They build up higher and higher, a thin layer coating the bottom of her window sill. The frozen wilderness outside makes the window pane cold to the touch as her warm palm rests against the glass.

She sniffles, though not from the cold, but instead from the tears that fall from her eyes and the tightness of her throat. Five months. Five months exactly since she saw Atlas for the last time. Five months of questions. Five months of pitiful looks. Five months of mourning.

It was hell, and Cally barely had the strength to continue. Every day she saw him, whether it was a pair of dark eyes she saw in passing, a flash of pale skin, or even just a tall frame with broad shoulders. Cally looked for him everywhere even though she knew she would never find him.

She opens her palm slowly, revealing the pearl he gifted to her. A splash of water lands on her open palm beside it, a tear that dripped from her nose. Cally wondered where he was, what he was doing, if he was thinking about her.

Had he moved on, or did he still grieve like she did?

A part of her wanted him to miss her, but at the same time she wouldn't wish this pain on anyone. The pain of knowing their love was lost forever, their passion separated by the sea itself.

She had once been a captive, yes, and though she was free now, a piece of herself was still held captive beneath those cerulean waves. A part of her soul would forever be attached to that of the man she loved with her entire being, and just the same a part of him was attached to her.

They had both left their mark on the other, each of them giving away a part of themselves that neither would ever get back. That's Love's way, you see. What is given is gone forever and no matter how you search to fill the gap, nothing will ever fit but the one who has the missing piece.

That was Cally's problem. She had happily given her entire soul to the dark eyed boy. A part of her heart was left with him that she would never get back. She was satisfied with this though, in that it kept the two forever tied. She would always be with him just as he would always be with her.

Cally guides the pearl to her lips, pressing a soft kiss to the little orb. Just then, a knock sounded at her door.

"Come in," she says, her voice hoarse.

The door opens to reveal one of the only faces that has been able to bring her joy these past months. "Hey, Ethan."

The little boy enters slowly, two steaming mugs of hot coco held in his small hands. Cally instantly rises to assist him. She takes her own mug and gestures for him to sit beside her in the window seat.

He smiles nervously at her, his little brows furrowing as he sees the evidence of her crying.

"Are you okay?" He whispers, as though someone might overhear.

"I'm alright," she says through a forced smile.

"You don't have to be scared anymore," he says. "Momma says I'm big and strong now. I can protect you."

Cally laughs softly, reaching over to fluff his blonde curls. The boy giggles and nearly spills his coco as he scrambles away.

It is silent after that, the two just watching the snow fall. The only sound is their own breathing and Ethan's slurps as he amateurly sips on his drink. Cally clutches the pearl tighter.

"Why are you still afraid?" Ethan suddenly asks. "You are home with us. You are safe now."

He was right. She was home and she was safe. But that wasn't what she feared.

No one really understood why Cally wept so much after her rescue. No doctors could figure out why she refused to speak of what happened to her. None truly understood her sadness and why she was so heartbroken. Atlas was hers to remember and the secret of his identity was one she would go to the grave with.

Or maybe... maybe she didn't have to. Maybe she could share his legacy. Maybe she coul share it with someone worthy enough to hear his testimony. Perhaps someone else knowing of their love was exactly what was needed.  Perhaps their tale must be told.

"Ethan?" The child looks up at his sister. "I'm going to tell you a story," she says. "A story about a boy named Atlas."

# Epilogue

-------------------------------------------------------------

The little boat glides easily over the calm sea. A practiced hand rotates the steering wheel, turning the bow in the desired direction. A wisp of grey hair is tucked behind an ear, grey hair once golden blonde. Weathered fingers clasp tightly around a necklace, a necklace with a pearl pendant.

It has been fifty years now. Fifty very, very long years, but they weren't all bad. The first few were the hardest. When Calliope first attended college, it was a struggle she wasn't quite prepared for. Any friends she met were always concerning themselves with boys, some with the intention of fun nights, others looking for spouses.

This separated Cally from the rest. They never understood why she didn't have any interest in men. They never knew why she refused every date she was offered. But how could they know? It wasn't easy to explain that her heart belonged forever to someone else.

It was not until after she graduated with her bachelors and was moving on with her masters in marine biology that things began to look up for Cally. The people she was around in those years were more like her, cared less about trivial love.

Perhaps that is why finding love came easier.

She met a man named Thomas in her final year of school. At first, she didn't think much of him, but his constant affection and obvious feelings for her soon made her accept his offer of a date. Cally liked him. She liked the man with the cute smile, fluffy brown hair and adorable glasses.

As things grew more serious between them, Cally became more and more depressed. She found herself slipping back into the grieving state of mind that had plagued her years before. She felt guilty for moving on, but she was also angry that she couldn't love Thomas like he deserved.

It was when Thomas proposed that Cally was forced to explain. She told him everything. She told him about her kidnapping, about Atlas, and about their love. At first he didn't believe her, and perhaps he never did, but he accepted it. Whether or not all of her story was true, Thomas knew that Cally's heart didn't truly belong to him. He knew that there was some lucky man out there who had managed to capture her love.

But he was alright with that.

Thomas told her that he would love her anyways, and that he would do his best to show her as much love as he could. He promised her a comfortable life and in return, Calliope accepted.

Cally was not home often in her early adulthood. After their marriage, Thomas and Cally spent many years traveling the world's many oceans and rivers. Their studies led them all across the globe as they researched any and all aquatic species.

It was not until Calliope became pregnant with their first child that they finally settled down. The young family moved to a comely home on the east coast where they lived the rest of their lives comfortably.

After forty years of marriage, Thomas grew ill. His heart began to fail and he passed quietly in his sleep from a heart attack. Cally mourned many months for him. The man who had been her companion for so long had left her and she felt very, very alone.

That was four years ago.

Cally's children were grown, her husband had passed on, and her home was empty. For most, it would be the time to move on, but for Cally, she decided it was time to go back.

The little boat continues onward in its trek and soon a small strip of land appears. As the sun begins to slope down, Cally finally arrives back at her true home.

The island looks much the same as it did those many years ago. The same rocks still lined the beach, the same trees still in their places, though much thicker than they had been. She runs the boat ashore, her aged body aching as she climbs down from it. Her joints don't work quite so well as they used to.

Cally kicks off her shoes and begins to walk down the familiar beach. As the sand sinks beneath her feet, a rush of memories resurfaces. So much happened here. So many wonderful, joyous memories. So many happy moments filled with laughter. So many days of young, tender love.

Cally walks slowly down the beach, reminiscing. But then she hears a voice, low and more gravelly than it once was, but still very, very familiar.

"Calliope."

She turns around to see him.

He looks very different, but still very much the same. He is still tall with the same lean build, but his skin isn't quite as healthy as it used to be. Wrinkles make his features harsh, his muscles not quite as strong as they once were. Grey hair is peppered through his once beautiful dark locks. But his eyes, oh his eyes are exactly what they always were. Piercing, sharp, alert, passionate.

"Atlas," she whispers.

Atlas didn't think he would ever hear that voice again.

That beautiful, delicate voice that sang to him so many years ago. It is lower than it was in her youth, but it is still hers.

She takes a small step towards him, hesitantly, almost as if she were afraid.

"I didn't think you would come back," Atlas admits.

"Neither did I," she replies honestly. "Atlas--"

Her knees buckle as the weight of her emotions become too much to bear. Atlas is there in an instant, catching her before she can hit the sand.

She is soft, much softer than she had been, he feels. Her hips are rounder, her stomach full and breasts larger and looser. The two sink down to the sand, Atlas holding her to his chest.

She cries softly as no words are spoken. No words need to be spoken. Each understood exactly what the other wanted to say. Atlas rests his chin on her head, his lips pressing into her hair--grey hair discolored by age--but that didn't matter. Her hair didn't need to be golden like it was for him to love it. It just needed to be hers.

Soon Atlas spotted the pearl pendant swaying from her neck. He raises it gently, catching her attention.

"You kept it," he says.

"Always," she admits. "I wear it always."

"Even after all this time?" He asks.

"Especially after all this time."

Atlas then reaches for her left hand, lifting it to reveal a small golden band encircling her left fourth finger. "What is this?"

Cally swallows. "That was my wedding ring."

"You married?" Atlas asks hesitantly, almost ready to let her go out of respect for the new man she had found.

"I did," she answers. "He cared for me very much, Atlas. But I--"

"But what?"

"I never forgot you," she whispers. "You were always the man I truly loved, Atlas. He knew that, though. We married knowing he could never fill your place."

"I didn't want that," Atlas mutters miserably. "I wanted you to find someone to love."

"I did. I found you, and you gave me all the love I could ever ask for. But Thomas... Thomas gave me everything else."

Atlas nods, rubbing her shoulders soothingly. "He is a good man, then. Can I... Can I meet him?"

Cally shakes her head. "He died four years ago."

He squeezes her shoulders comfortingly. "I'm sorry."

"It's alright," she sighs. "That's why I'm here, though. I have accomplished everything I wanted. I went to school, I made an impact with the research I did in marine biology, and I had my children, so now I've decided to come home."

Atlas smiles brighter than he had in a very, very long time. "You had children."

Cally nods against his chest, sitting up to fix him with her gaze. "I did. Three very beautiful children. Two girls named Scarlett and

Hanna after women in Thomas' family. Then I had a baby boy... a boy I named Atlas."

Atlas holds her cheek gently in his weathered palm. "You named him after me."

Cally only nods, tears of joy, nostalgia, and love streaming down her cheeks.

Atlas was over the moon. She had gotten everything she ever wanted, and he couldn't be more proud. All those years he longed to accompany her, but he knew it wasn't his place. She had found where she needed to be, found who she needed to be with. Her life was happy, and that was all Atlas ever wanted for her.

"I'm so proud of you, my love," he says. "I'm so proud of the woman you have become and all you were able to accomplish." All you were able to accomplish without needing me.

"I wanted you to be there," she admits. "It's selfish, but I wanted it to be you standing across from me on my wedding day. I wanted it to be you who took Scarlett to her first dance recital. I wanted to be you who was by my side when I named my son after you."

"But I was there," Atlas promises. "Do you not remember what I told you?" He lays his hand over her heart. "Do you not remember the love I gave you? Cally, you always carried a piece of me with you everywhere you went. You had my love--all the love I could give you."

"And I hope you know that you had mine," she whispers, resting her forehead against his.

Cally rests against Atlas' side, his arm wrapping loosely around her. It had been so many years, but their love was just as fresh--just as young--as it always was.

Cally lays her hand on his knee. "How long?" She asks.

"Tomorrow."

Calliope looks up at him, Atlas' dark eyes tenderly meeting hers. "I'm not leaving this time."